THE
BANSHEE
AND THE
BULLOCKY

Bill Scott was born in Bundaberg, Queensland in 1923. He has worked at many trades, both ashore and afloat, including service in the Royal Australian Navy from 1942 to 1946. He worked in publishing and bookselling for twenty-five years and has been a full-time author since 1974. He has published more than twenty books, mainly on Australian folklore and for children, and his poems and short stories are in many anthologies. In 1992 he was awarded the Medal of the Order of Australia for his work as a folklorist. He now lives in Warwick with his wife Mavis Scott, also a writer for children.

THE BANSHEE AND THE BULLOCKY
Tales of my Uncle Arch

BILL SCOTT
*illustrations by **Ron Edwards***

University of Queensland Press

First published 1996 by University of Queensland Press
Box 42, St Lucia, Queensland 4067 Australia

Text © Bill Scott 1996
Illustrations © Ron Edwards 1996

This book is copyright. Apart from any fair dealing
for the purposes of private study, research, criticism
or review, as permitted under the Copyright Act, no
part may be reproduced by any process without written
permission. Enquiries should be made to the publisher.

Typeset by University of Queensland Press
Printed in Australia by McPherson's Printing Group

Distributed in the USA and Canada by
International Specialized Book Services, Inc.,
5804 N.E. Hassalo Street, Portland, Oregon 97213-3640

Cataloguing in Publication Data
National Library of Australia

Scott, Bill, 1923– .
  The Banshee and the Bullocky: tales of my uncle Arch.

  I. Edwards, Ron, 1930– . II. Title.

A823.3

ISBN 0 7022 2775 7

For my mother

Contents

Acknowledgments *ix*

The Wooden-legged Cockatoos *1*
The Young Men's Revenge *7*
The Giant Earthworms *11*
The Giant Mozzies *17*
Charlie and Martha *27*
The Slippery Gully *33*
Aubrey and the French Flea *37*
John the Yabby *43*
The Crafty Barramundi *49*
The Cunning Cockroach *55*
Treacle Jimmy *63*
The Deadly Quicksand *69*
The Betoota Rum Festival *77*
The Great Sheepdog Trials *81*
The Giant Mud Gudgeon *87*
Cyril and the Termites *93*
Scotty, Maria, Onions, and the Dutchman *99*
The French Chef *103*
Uncle Arch and the Bower Bird *109*
The Two Sisters *115*
Great Uncle Angus *121*

Acknowledgments

Some of these stories were first published in the following magazines, to whom acknowledgment is made: *Overland, Makar, Australian Tradition, Queensland Folk, Windy Hill Press*, and *Reading 360*.

The Wooden-legged Cockatoos

If it hadn't been Arch who told me about it I'd never have believed it. It happened up near Bundaberg in the early days, before World War I. Things were crook and Grandad used to go away all the week navvying on the railway line, and work the farm at the weekends. The only crop they had in that year was four acres of corn, and it was ripening nicely, corn like you don't see nowadays — one cob was a feed for a dozen chooks — but things aren't what they were, Arch says. That's beside the point. The point was that a big mob of cockatoos had found the paddock and used to turn up for a feed around daylight every morning. They'd pick a couple of the mob to keep nit, then they'd hoe into the corn.

Cockatoos being what they were in those days, said my uncle, nearly the size of small scrub turkeys, they made an awful mess of the corn. Arch reckons you could hear the noise of their beaks at work from three hundred yards away, like clay going through a pugmill. Naturally, Grandad was wet as hell. Pushing a pumper home eleven miles on a Friday night didn't make him too happy to begin with, and when he found his only chance of settling with the storekeeper going down the crops of those sulphur-crested (birds) he was real cranky. He used to get up at daylight and take his old muzzle-loading shotgun away through the tea-trees down to the paddock, but those cockies were too shrewd for him and he'd come home soaked to the waist with dew and never blow so much as a feather off them.

The language he used when he was out of the hearing of Granny and the girls was something awful, Arch says.

2 The Banshee and the Bullocky

He says that his bullocks would never have worked nearly so well in later years if he hadn't remembered some of the things he'd heard his father call those cockatoos. That used to bring them up into their collars all right. They used to listen to him in a sort of unbelieving silence and then break tracechains. But that's beside the point.

The point is that one Sunday night, after a weekend spent scrambling through the wallum, he decided that as he'd have to get back up the line the following morning, the boys'd have to shoot the birds during the week. But cockatoos were more cunning in those days, and they used to wait until the bell rang for school in the morning and then settle on the corn and eat till the bell sounded for end of school in the afternoon, when they'd stagger away through the scrub and roost till the following day, smacking their beaks and muttering

appreciation. By the next weekend it was clear that unless Grandad could think of something pretty good there wasn't going to be any crop at all. So he came up with this idea.

It was no good trying to creep up on the birds. The sentries were too cunning for him. He tried it twice on the Saturday and all he succeeded in hitting with the old gun was a sparrow that, in exasperation, he blew into shreds of fluff. So late Saturday afternoon he double-charged the old gun with the black-grain powder, and topped her up with nails, tacks and ball until she was down in the front like a badly winded horse. He rammed in a wad of paper then off to the corn paddock. Like all schemes of genius his plan was simple yet foolproof. He lashed the gun to a fencepost with baling wire, so that the muzzle was aimed just over the tops of the corn. Then he explained the part that Arch tells me he didn't think much of. He was to sneak down to the paddock before daylight in the morning and hide in the middle of the corn. When the cockies landed he was to sing out at the top of his lungs and frighten the birds. From his hiding place Grandad would then pull the trigger with a piece of string, and as the frightened birds rose from their feeding the grapeshot would catch them between wind and water and sink them without trace. So Grandad reckoned. Arch was windy about it but Grandad said he had to have faith in his father's judgment, and anyway he'd belt him if he argued too much, so there was nothing Arch could do about it.

The next morning they hid as planned, and sure enough, down came the cockatoos. They settled and started to feed. Arch yelled and they rose. Grandad pulled the string. There was a noise like a blasting charge in a quarry, but when the smoke cleared away they found they hadn't got one cockatoo, and the recoil of the gun had knocked down the best part of a chain of fence. Grandad had been a fraction of a second late pulling the trigger. Just how close they came to shooting

them all down is shown by the fact that they picked up two sugar-bags of cockatoos' legs. They never saw the cockatoos again; but years later Arch heard of a mob of wooden-legged cockatoos down in the Northern Rivers of New South Wales that lived on nuts, fruit, and berries, and always flew around and never over corn paddocks.

The Young Men's Revenge

Once, a long time ago, my Uncle Arch was a young fellow, just the same as everyone else. Seems hard to realise when you look at him, but it's so. He was brought up on a quarter section selected by my grandfather just outside a little coastal town in Queensland. After he left school he used to work around the area, fencing on contract, chasing cockatoos, and learning to do all kinds of bush work that stood him in good stead all the years he was roaming round the countryside later on.

He used to knock round with a team of half-a-dozen other young fellows about his age, and they used to have to stir up their own fun, because they thought that things were a bit slow. The older people in the township used to reckon that the place was going to the dogs, and that young fellows were no good, and got things too easy; not like when they were young when they had to work real hard. The young fellows would do all sorts of daring things, like hobbling a bloke's horse while they were talking to him, so's he wouldn't notice until he tried to ride off. One night they changed all the gates in the township round on their hinges, and another night they swapped all the washing round on the clotheslines. Very reckless and daring in their misbehaviour, until the older people in the town all said that they needed a good lesson. But Arch and his mates didn't care.

The bloke that had it in for them most was a little skinny bloke who had a selection just outside town. Every year he used to plant melons in his corn paddock, and of course the young fellows woke up and they used to go out and pinch them. They were very fond of watermelon, but the main reason that they used to go and pinch them was so they could hear this bloke go crook. He was a little, skinny bloke called Perce Stanley, and he used to stand in the bar at the pub and he'd never look at you while he was going crook. He'd stand and stare into the bottom of his beer glass as though he was going crook at the froth.

Well, Perce tried all ways to stop those young blokes pinching his melons, from rat traps to a shotgun loaded with saltpetre. The boys were having a marvellous time dodging him and they kept it up to see if they could get him really ropeable. Perce'd sit up all night in his melon patch waiting for them and there wouldn't be a sign of them, but if he dozed off for a minute another melon would disappear. He got real cranky and took to firing an occasional blast into the tea-trees that surrounded the paddock, but he never even came near hitting any of the mob, and they used to laugh just loud enough for him to hear.

Well, they had Perce pretty near crotchety with their goings-on, and the melons kept disappearing one by one. Then Perce had an idea. He bought two pounds of Epsom salts at the grocers, and mixed it into a real strong solution in about a quart of water. Then he got a lampwick and off to the paddock. First he made sure that none of the young blokes were round, then he carefully slit the stem between the biggest melon and the vine. He wangled the lampwick into the slit, then dipped the other end of it into the solution of Epsom salts. By nightfall the melon had drunk all the Epsoms and seemed to have swollen to twice the size.

I told Arch this was called capillary attraction. He said he didn't care what it was called, after they pinched that melon and ate it in the dark the results were spectacular. Worse. Perce told everybody what he'd done and all the people in town started to laugh at the boys, and the sheilas wouldn't dance with them, and the older people got round saying that the young fellows still had a lot to learn. So Arch and his mates were determined to get their revenge.

Now, when Arch was a lad, you didn't go round blowing up letterboxes on Guy Fawkes night, like we used to do when I was a lad. They used to cut two long saplings in the scrub, and then a team of them would sneak round in the middle of the night. They'd slide the two poles under somebody's outhouse, then they'd all lift together and carry the building away, and leave it in somebody else's backyard. Well, this happened to be about Guy Fawkes time, so they thought they'd do a real good job of Perce's lavvy. About one o'clock in the morning of the fifth of November they slipped the two poles under Perce's rear building and carried it down to the other end of town and left it in the middle of the road outside the police station.

This mightn't seem such a wicked thing to have done, and the boys were all chuckling about it all night; but in the morning a certain amount of difficulty arose. You see, Perce had been at the pub the night before, celebrating his victory over those flaming youths; and he'd got pretty full.

About midnight he'd had to go up the yard for reasons of his own, and it being a warm night and no mosquitoes, he'd drifted off to sleep. Well, the door was shut, and the boys never noticed the extra weight when they shifted the building. The gentle swaying motion of the transportation rocked Perce into even deeper slumber. He didn't wake up until the kids going to school the next morning opened the door to see if there was anyone inside. Perce's difficulty was that he was such an old-fashioned bloke that he still favoured the flannel nightgown instead of the newfangled pyjamas, and so there he was, in his little retreat in the middle of the main street, and nobody would bring him a pair of pants until the constable woke up and lent him a pair of uniform trousers to go home in. There was room for about three blokes Perce's size inside the pants, and he looked a bit

10 The Banshee and the Bullocky

like a walking stick in a big brown paper bag on the way home. The constable went crook at him for carelessness and the people all laughed at him and he got ropeable, and went looking for the boys with a shotgun, and they all left town and got on the track. Arch went offsiding for a bullocky, and that's the way he came to leave home for the first time. Perce gave up trying to stop blokes from pinching his melons after that. He just used to plant half-an-acre more from then on, which I suppose he could have done in the first place. Poor old Perce, he died years ago, but I don't think he'll ever be forgotten.

The Giant Earthworms

My Uncle Arch was running a goldmine during the Depression years. It was called the Dead Goat and it was out in the back country near the Goodnight Scrub. It was very up and down sort of country; you had to lead your packhorse uphill and then follow him down the other side. It's steep country. I've often wondered why you had to do that with your packhorse, but there must have been a good reason for it or Arch wouldn't have done it. Arch says the ore was pretty good, it had to be to make it worth working because the stone carrying the gold was in little mullocky leaders through an enormous bed of clayey soil and you had to shift tons of overburden

to get a few hundredweight of stone. But he was managing to keep the wolf from the door, so he stuck at it though he couldn't afford to send the stone away for treatment. He used to burn it himself and then dolly it up and run it through a cradle.

One day he was working away when a skinny old bloke with a beard like a billy goat came up the ridge and wandering down the spur. It turned out that this bloke was a bug-hunter and he was hunting for a particular kind of worm that lived in those parts. You've all heard of those giant earthworms that grow three feet long. They come from Queensland and Victoria and there aren't any in New South, though what that proves I'm not sure. But that's beside the point. The point is that this bloke asked Arch if he'd seen any of them and Arch admitted that he was always coming across them while he was digging, following the leaders through the clay until they pinched out. So the old bloke asked Arch if he could camp there with him for a few days, so Arch said "Ribuck", an expression he'd picked up in France in 1917.

If you think I'm going to say the old bloke dug out the main reef while he was looking for worms, you're mistaken. He found lots of worms, and soon had eight of them oozing round in an old tank someone had left there. He half-filled it with soil and put some gauze over the top, and he used to sit there on a bucket turned upside down and just watch those worms. One night Arch asked him what he was watching for and the old bloke said he was studying them and that he hoped to see them breeding. Arch said that he didn't see that eight were necessary in that case, surely two were enough; but the old bloke said that in this case one would suffice as the worms were both male and female at the same time. This rocked Arch a bit, as you can imagine, and as he explained to me if he hadn't known a woman who kept a boarding-house in France in 1917 who was like that he would have thought the old bloke was having a go at him.

At any rate the old bloke went through about four days later, having filled four notebooks on both sides of the page, leaving Arch the worms and the tank. Arch forgot about them until four days later, when it occurred to him that it might be a good idea to let the poor beggars go. Arch is a kindly man and friendly to all animals. By this time the worms were a bit hungry, having worked over the soil in the tank pretty thoroughly; so he thought he'd give them a bit of a treat before letting them go. He tossed them a half a tin of plum jam that had gone a bit mouldy, then turned them loose. Didn't they just wire into that jam! They'd never tasted anything as good as that before, and to his amazement they began turning up at his tent every morning after that and he used to give them a teaspoon of jam each.

They got so tame and friendly that Arch began to wonder if he couldn't teach them a few tricks. There was one big one in particular that caught on very quickly. It watched him panning off the cradle one day and putting the gold in the pickle bottle. Next morning when they turned up for their jam bless me if the worm didn't have a little slug of gold in his mouth. Arch used to call this worm Stumpy because he didn't know what else to call it. You couldn't call it Joe or Dave or Emily or Susan or anything like that. Not that it made any difference, it all came to the same thing in the end. Anyhow he gave Stumpy two spoons of jam instead of one and the other worms soon took a wake-up. Next morning they all brought him a slug of metal. It was pathetic, Arch reckons, how they'd come wriggling across the flat with their little beady eyes shining trustfully up at him and a couple of weights in their gobs. Soon they were bringing him more gold than he could dig himself, so he took things easy, and sat around the camp boiling the billy now and then, and the next time he went to the store he came home with a case of plum jam.

14 The Banshee and the Bullocky

It was round about this time that this dirty big jackass came to live on the ridge. Now, as I said before, Arch is a friendly man and kind to all beasts except maybe Joe Blakes, so he didn't mind the jackass much. He even used to chuck it a bit of damper or a bit of fat off the back of the salt beef, until one morning only six worms showed instead of eight and the jackass didn't bother to show at all. Of course Arch woke straight away what was happening but he couldn't seem to stop that bird. To cut a long story short and not bore you with the yarn of how him and the bird tried to outwit each other, the odds stood that the jackass was missing some plumage and the only worm left was Stumpy. Stumpy was a wreck. The poor fellow was worn out from diving down holes and looking back over his shoulder. He ran himself ragged, said Arch, in an effort to help his human friend. To show how he appreciated the effort Stumpy was making he gave Stump a whole tin of jam to himself one morning. This was the downfall of all his hopes. Stumpy just couldn't stand it and he died of indigestion.

Arch says there wasn't much he could do about it. He felt that he couldn't bear to stay in a place that had such sad memories for him so he rolled his drum and headed west. The jackass ate Stumpy's remains and I'm delighted to say died of a plum-stone that stuck in its vitals. That, said Arch, is why to this day he can't abide plum jam. He's too sentimental. Quite apart from the fact that that's the only sort of jam they ever got to eat in France in 1917.

The Giant Mozzies

My Uncle Arch had a team of bullocks once that could climb like goats and pull like traction engines. They were those big-shouldered wide-horned roans with purple eyes that you don't see round the place any more. They were so fit that any one of them could pull his own weight up a wall. Arch says the last team that he saw that was anyways like it was the one they used to pull the clock up the City Hall tower in Brisbane after all the tractors had got bogged because they'd built the place in a swamp. That's beside the point, of course. What we were talking about was this team that Arch used to have. He was using them wagoning freight up from Brisbane to the Gympie diggings, and one particular trip he got the contract to pull a big Lancashire boiler

weighing eleven tons three hundredweight two quarters up to the new stamp mill they were building near Monklands. The trip was a bit of fruit for a team like Arch's, except for the Blackall Range. That's a bit of up and down country near Eumundi, but it wasn't the grades that had Arch worried. It was the mosquitoes.

You all know mozzie stories. There's some whoppers in New Guinea, I'll admit. There's some beauties in the vine scrub between Tully and Kuranda that I've bumped myself a few times. They aren't so much huge as agile. I'm told a bloke called Ironbark Bill had a bit of bother with a team down the Northern Rivers way. But according to Arch these are all only the inbred degenerate descendants of a race that reached their full flower along the Maroochy River and in the wallum country south of Double Island Point. They kept a lookout in a dirty big ironbark tree on top of Mount Tibrogargan, and men passing through that country used to circle their camps with cowdung fires and sit up all night with double barrel shotguns loaded with grapeshot if they didn't want to wake up in the morning as empty as a boundary rider's pockets after a week in a Brisbane pub. They were as intelligent as they could be, those mozzies, and as soon as the mozzie who was keeping nit spotted anything moving toward the foot of the ridges, he'd shadow it until he saw where it was, then he'd sprint back to report to the chief mozzie who'd get them all organised to attack as soon as darkness fell.

They were a tough mob, all right. They drank citronella and used flyspray for aftershave lotion. They dusted their armpits with DDT powder. They reckoned it kept the fleas down. But they weren't as tough as Arch, and this had been driven home to them a few years previously when they tried to knock off a straggler from a herd of elephants Arch was droving through for Jimmy Tyson. He gave them such a doing over that time that it cured them of ever wanting to interfere with him again. They weren't real scared but they respected him, if you understand. Whenever the sentry saw him coming the whole mob of them used to fly inland and roost round Kingaroy for a week until he was out of their area.

Even though he knew he had the wind up them Arch used to start looking out as soon as he reached the foot of the Belli Pass. He never passed a night in that district without chaining the bullocks to the wagon so they couldn't be carried off in the night. He was always kind to animals, and anyway the bullocks were so fond of him that he didn't want to lose any of them. (I boggled a bit over this part of his story because once in my youth I heard him talking to a team, but he maintained that there wasn't any other way you could talk to a bullock and keep its respect and affection.)

At any rate, what Arch didn't allow for this time was that the mozzie doing cockatoo duty this particular day was a young mozzie who had never met Arch, only heard of him. Another thing, while he was in Brisbane Arch had been to the barbers and had his whiskers trimmed from a Royal Flush down to a set of Dundrearies. So when this young mozzie saw him coming from the top of Mount Tibrogargan he thought Arch was just another Choom, and didn't he lick his chops when he saw all those fat beasts. Waiting until Arch was in a dip of the ground and couldn't see him, he took off and glided all the way back to camp so he wouldn't be heard. He told all the other mozzies about this new-chum colonial experience man he'd just spotted and they got ready to do the team over that night.

Well, Arch camped that night at the top of the Belli, and he's the first to admit that he was careless. Of course he circled the camp with dung fires and chained the team to the wagon after they'd picked a bit of grass, but he went to sleep. The mozzies, still not knowing it was him, swung into action. One team landed upwind from the fires and fanned with their wings. This blew the smoke away. In the meantime a selected team of very muscular mozzies swooped in and fastened onto the team and started to fly away with them. Wasn't there a row when the chains brought them up short! Those mozzies were powerful but they couldn't manage the team and the wagon, not to mention the boiler. The roaring of their wings woke Arch. He jumped out of his blanket and yelled. Of course as soon as the mozzies recognised him they panicked. Something had to give and what gave was the chains holding the boiler to the wagon. It tumbled to the ground. This lightened the dray so much that the frantic mozzies were able to lift it; and Arch was horrified to see his twenty-four bullocks go sailing off, followed by the wagon.

There wasn't a thing he could do about it. There he was, at the top of the Belli Pass, with the boiler and nothing to carry it on. He could only make a billy of tea, and sit round waiting for daylight, talking to himself. When the mozzies got back to their camp they held a meeting straight away. The ones who had clashed with Arch over the elephant wanted to take the team and wagon back straight away and apologise, but there were a lot of young lair mozzies who were too young to remember and they were all hungry. These finally talked the older ones down and they held a barbecue on the spot. But a grey old mozzie was heard to remark thoughtfully as he picked his teeth with the wagon tongue, "Ah doot we've heard the last o' yon ploy!" And so it was. We'll come to that a bit later on. What I started out to tell you first was how Arch got the boiler to Gympie, and he had to do that or lose his contract.

He sat beside the fire, and drank tea, and thought. It was only about thirty-odd miles to Monklands, which wasn't very far, but it was too big a boiler for him to manage on his own. Then, all of a sudden, it hit him. Boiler! Boils! He remembered how when he had boils once, his old mother drew them with bread poultices. He built up the fire and by piccaninny daylight he had made the biggest bread poultice ever seen in the State of Queensland. This he applied to the end of the boiler.

The poultice drew so hard that he had to trot to keep up with it, and he got to Monklands in five hours and a quarter and over some pretty rough country too, stopping only to lend a bit of poultice to a horse team bogged in a creek crossing. He sold the remains of the poultice to a sawmill, where it worked for years pulling logs up a ramp until it wore out finally. This money, with the cheque he got for the boiler job, gave him just enough money to buy another team and wagon, but before he bought them he decided to go back down to the Maroochy and have his revenge on the mozzies. As I've mentioned, Arch is a kindly man with a lot of consideration for animals, but whenever he thought of his twenty-four big roans and how they'd gone to line the bellies of that mob of mozzies he got ropeable.

There were all sorts of things he could have done, of course. He thought about putting Epsom salts into the swamp where they went for a drink when they got dry. He thought about putting bindi-eyes in their beds. He thought about all sorts of things, but there didn't seem to be anything that occurred to him that would make them suffer in the way he wanted them to suffer. He considered asking a friend of his, a Mr E. Kelly up from his property in the Weddin Mountains in Victoria, to give him a hand, but Mr Kelly was busy at the time and Arch was never a man to interfere with another man's enjoyment. In the finish he decided to go off in the general direction of Maroochy and settle the mozzies himself, using whatever means came to hand.

He left Gympie early in the morning, and he'd only gone ten miles and a bit when he heard the most awful noise he'd ever heard in his life. At first he thought it was a dozen bullock drays and the bullockies hadn't put any fat on the axles. Then he thought it might be a bunyip he used to know out in the Territory come in to the coast. He knew it wouldn't be a local bunyip, because they'd all headed outback when nobody believed in them any more. It's tough when no one believes in you any more, and everybody goes round proving you're only a seal or a big water snake, or anything. Bunyips are sensitive, and the one Arch knew was no exception. As it explained to Arch, could it help it if its natural food was people. "Nobody goes round going crook at bees for eating honey", it used to say, bitterly. "They all say it's the bees' natural food. So why should everybody go round pickin' on bunyips, because they eat their natural food?" That's all beside the point, but I bet you hadn't thought about it in that light before.

The point is that Arch could hear this horrible noise coming through the scrub towards him, and he got a bit worried. He sneaked into a hollow log and waited. Not that he was frightened, says Arch. He was just being cautious, the way everybody is when they hear a noise like that in the bush for the first time. Anyhow, he saw this sheila coming up the track towards him, and he has to admit that she was one of the most striking looking women he had ever seen in his life. She had on this long flowing kind of robe and in those days when most women wore bustles and other things it was most unusual to see a sheila wearing a long flowing sort of robe, especially if they are dripping wet as well like this one was. Well, Arch got out of his log to have a better look, and the sheila spotted him and stopped the noise she'd been making, because Arch was a fine figure of a man in those days, he tells me. She sort of stood in the middle of the track, and pushed the hair over her eyes and pretended not to see him, though he could see she was peeping through the hair. So he went up to her and said, "Did you fall in the creek, lady?"

Well, when Arch asked her this it seemed to stiffen her a bit, and she asked him if he'd seen a bloke around by the name of Tim Grogan. Arch had to admit that he'd never seen this bloke, and the sheila got downhearted and sat down on a log and said in a Mick accent, "Sorra the day I left the old sod." Before Arch could get a chance to ask who the old sod was she started to tell him her tale of woe, and it was a pip. She admitted that she was a Banshee, hailing from County Kerry, and she was known as the Curse of the Grogans. It seems that before a Grogan can snuff it he has to hear her. Arch asked her if it was the noise she'd been making, and she admitted that she'd been practising as she came along. It seemed that this Tim Grogan was the last Grogan left in Australia, and as soon as he snuffed it she could go back to Ireland and take up her residence in the old family peatbog again. Around this time he noticed that though she'd been sitting on the log in the sun for about a quarter-of-an-hour talking to him, she was as wet as ever; and that the water was sort of oozing out of her from inside and that she hadn't fallen in the creek at all. Well, he got a bit windy, but he had an idea and so he propositioned the sheila like this. If she would give him a hand with the mozzies, he'd scout round Gympie for this Tim Grogan for her. She thought about it for a while, then agreed.

Arch always lays his plans carefully, and this time was no exception. The first thing he did was to go into Gympie and get a bag of sugar. He slung this on his back and headed for the mozzies' main camp. The mozzies were away for the day, cleaning up a mob of sheep out at Dalby, so he had a clear go. The first thing he did was to cook up the sugar into the biggest pot of vinegar toffee ever seen in those parts. While it was still hot he painted it all over the ground where the mozzies used to camp at night. Of course it set hard and glossy in the sun, but Arch knew that as soon as the dew fell at sundown it would go all sticky; and if you blokes think there is anything in the world stickier than vinegar toffee you have never taken your kids to a church fete. He planted the Banshee in a nearby patch of scrub, and explained his plan, so she'd have no trouble swinging into action at the right moment. Then, for good measure, he put a sack of Epsoms in the drinking water anyway. Then he planted himself in another patch of scrub on the other side of the clearing and waited patiently for sundown.

The mozzies came planing in, picking their teeth with saplings and arguing about what they'd do the next day. It was a peaceful scene as they settled down for the night, and they didn't notice the toffee. In an hour there wasn't a mozzie left awake, not one. The dew fell and the toffee melted. The mozzies' feet sank into it, but as they were all asleep they didn't notice. Then Arch gave the lady a nod and she started her performance. At the same time Arch started to sing "Mother Mochree" from the bushes on the other side of the camp. The mozzies woke up, of course, and their first impulse was to gain height and look the situation over. They didn't get a look in. The toffee stretched a bit, but it held. Then the Banshee came out of the bushes and the more superstitious of the mozzies nearly gave themselves hernias trying to get off the ground. But the final horror was still to come.

Arch was through the first verse of "Mother Mochree"

by this and starting on the chorus. You know that real high bit on the first word of the last line of the chorus? Well, though he's very talented in many ways, and a kindly man, I reckon Arch would have the crookest voice between here and wherever he happens to be just now. You know what it's like at a party and a mob of you are all singing "Mother Mochree" and everybody has a go at that top note and nobody makes it? Well, Arch wasn't in the hunt of making it any more than you are. The sound that tore the air was so horrible that even the Banshee went for cover. It terrified the mozzies so much that they all took off together but the toffee was so sticky that it was the ground that gave way. There's been a chain of waterholes there ever since. The mozzies just kept going, and they reached about to Innisfail before they flew into a rain squall that melted the toffee and the ground fell away from their feet. They kept going, though, until they reached New Guinea, and some of their descendants live there yet. Ask any of the blokes who were up there during the war. The Banshee never went home to Ireland. Arch went and scouted for Tim Grogan, but he couldn't find him. The Banshee ended up housekeeping for a gang of railway fettlers outside Alice Springs. She's a godsend to them, with her talent for moisture. She waters their vegetable garden for them.

Tim Grogan made his pile on the Palmer, and retired to live in County Kerry forty years ago. And he's still living there, though with the politics and the censorship and one thing and another he's beginning to go crook that the Banshee hasn't been round to see him. Arch went banana bending on contract just after this, but I'll tell you about this some other time.

Charlie and Martha

My Uncle Arch was walking down the main street in Innisfail once, years ago before they had streetlights, and he fell over a blackfellow who had gone to sleep on the ground. Now this blackfellow was an old bloke, who used to sleep there before there was any town, and he didn't see why he should give up his bed just because a lot of silly white fellows had built humpies there. After all, he'd been there first. Also, he was the second best local witchdoctor, and was used to a certain amount of respect from the locals and he certainly wasn't used to blokes putting their big feet in his breadbasket in the night. So he got cranky. He didn't even give Arch time to apologise, not that Arch was thinking about apologising at the time because he had gone feet over head into a dirty big patch of sensitive plant that dug him full of prickles. Naturally he had lifted his voice in his best manner the same way he did to his bullocks the night they got a fright and ran over his camp. Anyhow the old blackfellow listened to him for a while after he got his own breath back, then he said that since Arch sounded like a flying fox in a fig tree he might as well look like one too, so he said a few words in his own language and bless my heart and soul if Arch didn't turn into a flying fox on the spot.

As you might imagine, Arch was a bit taken aback. One minute there he was on the ground picking bits of sensitive plant out of himself and the next minute he was hanging by his feet to the top branch of the big mango tree over the road. There was another flying fox called Charlie on this branch already and he was eating a mango, and when he saw Arch land he got cranky too. Everybody was cranky that night.

"Blankety blank dash blank," said Charlie. "You got the whole blanking tree to dash land in and you blanky dash dash dash have to land near me. Go and find your own mangoes, you shocking cross between a bandicoot and a hooky-handled umbrella." All flying foxes talk like that all the time.

Arch was a bit taken aback by being spoken to like that by a bloke he had never met before, so he went along the branch and belted the other flying fox in the belly, remarking as he did so ...

"Cop that, you pointy-toothed barrel-bellied squinty-eyed little misfit."

The other flying fox just hung there wheezing for a minute, then he said, "Well, blank me. You ain't one of our blanky mob. Where are yer from, mate?"

Arch told him that he came from the Goodnight Scrub near Mount Perry, but he didn't admit to being human. He knew that flying foxes didn't like humans because the Aborigines used to eat them. "Same like chooky," they said. Arch finished up getting pretty matey with this Charlie, and got invited to go home with him afterwards to the local camp, which was in a mangrove swamp down near Flying Fish Point. Just before daylight they took off.

I asked Arch what it felt like to fly and he said it was a bit like swimming and a bit like cracking a bullock whip with both hands at the same time, but that it was no problem if you had wings and kept your mind on what you were doing. When Arch and Charlie got to the swamp there were about two hundred other flying foxes there, and thousands more were flying in all the time. Some were sleeping, some were hanging there fanning themselves with their wings to keep cool. Some were abusing their husbands or wives or children or neighbours. Others of them just seemed to be hanging there not doing anything in particular except yell abuse at anybody that flew near them. Arch says that the noise was dreadful. He said that the only noise he ever heard like it was at a Sunday School picnic once when the word got round that the ice-creams were on at the other end of the park.

At any rate, him and Charlie landed on this mangrove tree and straight away all the other foxes that were hanging there already started to abuse them. Charlie just said, "Ah, get blocked, yer whingein' blanks, or I'll job yers. An' you better leave this blank alone or he'll job yers as well," which shut them all up except for one big fat lady flying fox who came swaying down the branch upside down and stared hard at Arch for a minute or two.

Then she said, "Well, I'll be blanked. You're not a bad-lookin' sort of a blanket. You'll do me for a mate. I been a shockin' widow too long. Three weeks since that dash green python ate me husband. How about it, good-lookin'. Want to be in it?"

Arch said to me that it was his experience that lady flying foxes had much the same sort of ideas as women but that they just don't bother to be as tactful because they are far more frank and direct, which at least gave you more chance because they weren't as deceitful as human women. In fact I had to interrupt him to get him back to the story. I'll tell you about the time he nearly got married some other time. He has never forgotten that experience, and is a bit inclined to dwell on it whenever he remembers it.

At any rate, it was his mate Charlie told the fat lady flying fox, "Ah, nick off, Martha, an' give 'im a go. The poor bustard ain't got his breath back. Come back later, a lot blanky later, yer silly old bag."

Well, she growled a bit but she went. Now Arch was worried about two things: the danger of a fate worse than death from Martha was bad enough, but this talk of a green python worried him even more. Charlie reckoned the snake was even worse than a blackfellow when it came to gobbling flying foxes. At last him and Charlie settled down to sleep for the day, but Arch had trouble getting to sleep, what with keeping one eye out for Martha and the other eye peeled for the green python. He dropped off at last, however.

He was wakened by a terrible racket. There were flying foxes going round and round the swamp at a terrific rate, all shouting language like you normally only read in best-selling novels, and on the branch about three feet away from him was the biggest and greenest python he had ever seen. It was looking at him in a most peculiar fixed way and it was saying in a dreamy sort of way, "Look into my eyes. You are growing drowsy ... sleep ... sleep ... sleep ...," and things like that. Arch was terrified because he knew that the green python was hypnotising him. He knew about people being hypnotised because he had once been a sideshow barker in a travelling circus and had got on to friendly rum-drinking terms with the bloke who did the hypnotising in the sideshow, and this bloke had taught him how to hypnotise people. So Arch was a wake-up to what this green python had in mind and he started to go into his own act that had made him famous in the northwest as the only bloke who ever managed to get a free drink from the teetotal publican at Flogger's Creek.

It took him five minutes of desperate mental effort to get that python under his spell. Then he told it that it was a bit of kangaroo hide lacing and got it to plait itself around the branch of the tree as though it was a whip-handle. When it was finished there was about a foot of each end of it left sticking out of the tangle, so he quickly tied the ends in a reef knot, which any boy scout can tell you will never slip under any circumstances. Then he woke it up. Of course it was terribly cranky, but there wasn't much it could do about it, and Arch became the hero of all the flying foxes in the area of the camp. But there was an awful fate still in store for him, because as saviour of the flying foxes in the tree he found that he was now automatically married to all the unattached ladies, who promptly started to form a queue on the branch, with Martha in first place. Arch was backing away down a limb that was getting bendier and bendier when he heard a human voice sing out to him and he was terribly relieved, on looking down, to see it was his old mate Black Peter, who had happened to be the best witchdoctor in the locality, and who was able to rescue him from his predicament in the nick of time.

Which is why Arch always carries a hurricane lamp around with him at night now, and whenever he sees a fat lady flying fox go past he always yells out, "G'day, Martha", and laughs like hell.

The Slippery Gully

My Uncle Arch was bullock-driving once on the Tablelands near Millaa Millaa, snigging logs out of gullies.

His offsider was a long inconsiderable streak of a bloke called Sandy Blight, because his name was Blight and he didn't hear very well. Arch used to talk to him pretty much by sign language, though he reckoned Sandy could hear a cork being pulled out of a bottle at two hundred and thirteen paces. Sandy had a good flow of language, though not as good as Arch. The bloke who taught Arch to swear was one of the old masters. He died very tragically. He was taking a team out of a creek crossing once when he got the hiccups unexpectedly and strangled in the flow of his own language. But that's beside the point.

The point is that the timber-cutters felled this big cedar, and it was a fair sort of tree even for those days. Took two men three days to chop it down, and then took ten minutes to fall. Arch says you don't often see trees like that any more. That's probably true.

Anyway, they trimmed the big stick where it lay and then cut it into sections with crosscut saws. Arch and Sandy got it onto the jinker by digging a hole under it and pushing the jinker in. Then they dug the earth out from under the ends and the log was loaded. Arch led the team down, and hitched them to the pole, and away they went.

Now, there had been a bit of rain the previous night, and the ground was a bit sticky and slippery, but these bullocks weren't ordinary bullocks, but relatives to the mob Arch lost years before to a team of mozzies. The tracechains rang like bells, but the wagon came up out of the hole and they set off for the main road to the railway. The railway was just being built, those days, and there was a big camp of navvies near the siding where they unloaded. But the real pinch for the team was a clay gully about three chains from the navvies' camp. Arch reckons it was so mucky that he once saw three ducks get bogged in it. What they used to do was this — they'd run like hell down the steep side, with the bullocks going at the gallop to stay ahead of the load, and the jinker would be halfway up the other side before the beasts had to start pulling. This usually got them through, but this was a big log they had aboard this time.

When they got to the top of the bank Arch pulled them up to give them a breather before making a rush for it. Sandy was especially cranky. He'd been on the rum the night before and forgot where he'd planted his heart starter so he was dry and hungover. Like an old smoke-dried corpse he was, in his flannel shirt, dungarees, and size ten blucher boots. Arch says he tried to explain to him about the run down and up by sign language because Sandy hadn't been through the gully in wet weather before, but it was hard to make contact with him somehow. His eyes were open, and his legs and voice were moving, but that was about all you could say for him. Still, the train was waiting so they had to go.

Arch gave a yell and the bullocks gave a tug. The jinker teetered over the edge and then started to go downhill like a mob of blokes at a party when the word goes round that the keg's been tapped. The bullocks pelted like hell to keep ahead and Arch and Sandy sprinted along, both encouraging the team. But when they hit the soft patch at the bottom the wagon stopped dead. The team kept going, because they broke the tracechains. Just as well, too, because the log kept going also, from momentum. Arch and Sandy just went into the mud to the knees and stuck. The team reached the top of the bank and pulled up for another breather, but the log didn't quite make it. It seemed to hesitate at the top, and then gravity took over and it began accelerating back down the slope.

Now, Arch could see it was going to miss him and the wagon, but it was headed straight for Sandy. Sandy didn't see it coming. He seemed to be listening for something. Arch yelled at him, but he took no notice. Arch couldn't get out of the mud either. The huge log was almost on top of Sandy when he suddenly jumped out of his boots and ran off towards the navvies' camp so fast that he seemed just to flicker, then vanish. The log crushed his boots out of existence a minute or two later.

What had happened, Sandy told Arch afterwards, was that he suddenly remembered where he'd left his bottle planted for the hair of the dog. He'd never noticed the log or anything else, being wrapped in his hangover. So Sandy was safe. But Arch was still stuck, and the log was now belting back down the slope towards him again. Fortunately his bullocks loved him, and threw him the end of the chain and pulled him out in the nick of time, though he was always taller and skinnier afterwards.

He left the log there, still sliding backward and forward. He'd nearly forgotten about it when he passed that way six months later, and there it was, still rolling up and down, though by this time the friction had worn it down to about the size of a skewer.

You might think Arch was pulling my leg but he proved the story was true. He picked up that bit of wood and he's kept it all these years. He showed it to me.

Aubrey and the French Flea

There were sixteen of us living on this old sheepdog at the time, and we had things pretty soft. We were all camped on his rump, just at the base of his tail where he couldn't reach us. He wasn't that good to eat, but you can't have everything, and I've tasted worse, like that time I was out in the Simpson Desert and had to live for a fortnight on marsupial mole. None of you young fleas know what that's like. Every time I opened my mouth I got a mouthful of sand. But that's beside the point. The point is we had it pretty soft, living on this dog. He was too old to do any mustering any more, so they just kept him at the homestead and used him for drafting round the yards. The rest of the time he spent sleeping in his hollow log or just outside the kitchen door. There weren't enough of us to bother him much. We looked at it this way: we gave him some sort of an interest in life and stopped him from getting too old and stiff. It was a bit of exercise for him, in a gentle sort of way, that kept up his muscle tone and helped his arthritis. On the other hand, he provided us with food and shelter in a quiet neighbourhood; none of that racing round in the sun and dust at the edge of a mob all day and then swimming round in a billabong so you had to hang on to your nose and hold your breath. Not that I haven't done that, in my younger days when I was droving, but when you get older you go more for comfort and a quiet life.

At any rate we're all sitting round on this dog's backside one day in the sun outside the kitchen door. The dog was asleep and we were just sitting there and nobody was saying very much, pretty drowsy, when the cook opened the door to sweep out the dust. The old dog must have thought there was going to be some tucker going because he levered himself to his feet and wandered over, looking up at the cook and pretending that he loved him. But the cook was busy and let the screen door slam shut. The dog was too lazy to walk back to his bush, and so he just slumped down in the shade of the washbench with the tin dish on it. Here the ground was damp and cool where someone had emptied the washing water.

We were just settling back to a doze when we heard this voice very faintly, but coming closer. It was yelling, "'Allo! Mes amis!"

Presently this very suave-looking continental-type flea came threading his way through the hair until he saw us. None of us answered him or anything — we didn't want any foreigners coming to live on our dog — but this didn't seem to bother him any. He just settled down and started to make himself at home as though he had a perfect right to come and share our home. We gave him the cold shoulder, but there's some people in this world that are so vain they don't realise you are ignoring them and snubbing them, and this flea was one of them. He thought we were shy and admiring such a voyaging bloke as himself, a real international flea.

I couldn't repeat to you some of the stories he told us about the dogs and people he'd lived on and the places he'd been on them and some of the things he boasted about used to make us old bush fleas blush. He'd come outback on a French governess the boss's wife had flown out to teach her daughters. Not that the daughters were anything to interest a flea; I've tried both of them at one time and another and I'd rather have an old sheepdog any day. But that's beside the point. The point is that this bloke used to sit round telling these immodest stories all the time until he made a lot of the young fleas blush, and one or two of them left the dog to find a home somewhere else. You couldn't shame him either. Old

Two-up, who lived on a dog that a girl in Mount Isa used to keep her feet warm, tried to talk him down, and there wasn't much he hadn't seen in his time; but this bloke was so vain that Two-up's yarns seemed only to spur him on to worse and worse stories. It was getting so that some of the rest of us were thinking about rolling our swags and moving out of the place we'd come to regard as a sort of eventide home, when this day the bullock team came up with the stores, and I was delighted to see it was driven by an old bloke I'd seen around before called Arch. Arch had a dog called Charles, and Charles had a flea called Aubrey whose mother had had pretensions to gentility; not that that made much difference to Aubrey. You see, it was like this.

This old bloke Arch was a pretty shrewd sort of bloke and so his dog Charles had sort of got to be pretty cunning too from watching him in action. Living on Charles as he did, Aubrey was full of wisdom, and was one of the most widely respected fleas in western Queensland. I knew he'd be coming over to visit us for a yarn and a change of diet, and I reckoned that if anybody could put the kybosh on this French New Australian flea it'd be Aubrey.

That night, sure enough, who should come bounding along but our old mate. Aubrey was a very active middle-sized flea, and mature and sensible as well. You could see that from his long sidewhiskers he sported, just beginning to go a dignified grey. He didn't have much to say for a while, couldn't get a word in really because this French flea was going on about how he had a market in a place called Paris named after an ancestor of his. I could see Aubrey taking all this in and frowning slightly, and when this bloke got started on his risky tales, I knew he was for it because Aubrey smiled. Waiting for a chance to get a word in edgeways, he said to me, "The giant fleas are thick this year."

That shut the other bloke up, and I could see him prick up his ear. "Giant fleas. Monsewer?" he asked politely, and I knew he must be impressed because he'd never been so polite and smarmy to anybody before.

"Yair," said Aubrey, and went on talking to me, not taking any notice.

"Monsewer," said the other bloke, "You are obviously one of our tiny and active species who has seen somewhat of the world. I would beg of you to enlighten me, a poor immigrant to your great country. Tell me of these, our great relations, of which you have spoken." I'd never heard him be so polite to anybody before.

"Ah, them," said Aubrey. "You don't want to worry about them. Know-all beggars. Reckon they've seen everything. I wouldn't go near them myself."

"Are they then dangerous, monsewer?" said the French flea, smiling with just a bit of a sneer. Anybody could see how brave he was just by looking at him.

"Ah, I wouldn't say dangerous," said Aubrey, meditatively. "More like big skites. Reckon they've been everywhere and seen the lot, that's all."

"I have not encountered them in Europe," said the French flea.

"Europe? Where's Europe?" asked Aubrey.

The French flea was quiet for a while but you could hear his mind turning over. The rest of us didn't know what to say, so we didn't say anything. After a while the New Australian flea spoke again. "Monsewer, I find it in me a great desire to encounter these great relatives of ours. It may be that I could learn much of them, and also, of course, tell them of my encounters in the great world of adventures."

"That's easy fixed," said Aubrey. "We'll be off again when the stores are off and the wool's on the wagon. Be my guest on my dog for a day or two and I'll drop you off where you can call on them."

"Thank you, monsewer," said the French flea.

"Think nothing of it," said Aubrey, and he hopped off, shouting over his shoulder. "I'll let you know when we're ready to leave."

About twelve months of peaceful life later, Aubrey came back with the drayload of stores and came over to visit as usual. We were all watching to see if the other bloke was with him, but he wasn't.

After a while, when we'd said good day, and had a feed, I said to him, "Whatever happened to the French flea?"

"Oh, him," said Aubrey. "You should have seen his face the first time he saw an old man kangaroo. The last I saw of him he was headed for the West Australian border, trying to tell the roo about his travels and wondering why it wasn't taking any notice of him. Is there any more tea in the billy?"

John the Yabby

Years ago my Uncle Arch was sitting in his humpy in the Goodnight Scrub when he thought he'd like to do a bit of saltwater fishing. He decided he'd go down and visit a couple of mates of his who lived at the mouth of the Kolan River, down on the coast. He didn't have a horse at the time so he walked. When he got tired of walking he ran for a while. He came east through Mount Perry and Gin Gin and Bullyard and then struck north until he came to the river and followed it down to the coast. That's where his two mates lived. They were called John the Yabby and Mulletgut Olaf.

Now, down in the Antarctic south of Australia, along the Murray and Murrumbidgee and other such shivering streams, they have a shellfish they call a yabby, but he's really only a kind of freshwater lobster. We have them in Queensland, too, only they grow bigger. For instance, you never heard of the southern ones digging their own waterholes, have you? But that's beside the point. The point is, as any Queensland fisherman can tell you, that a yabby is a sort of saltwater crayfish with claws, that looks as though someone has stepped on it. They have one huge enormous claw for fighting one another and a little skinny claw for eating with. They live in little holes they dig in the tidal mudflats, and the whiting love them. In fact you can even see whiting come out of the water at low tide and run round on the mud trying to catch them. At least you could at the mouth of the Kolan River forty years ago, Arch reckons. If you had a good blue cattledog you didn't even have to throw a line into the water. But that's beside the point.

They used to call Arch's mate John the Yabby because he fell into a circular saw in a pine mill once when he was full, and lost the best part of his left arm. His right arm had got very powerful in consequence. He had an old dinghy he used to scull round one-handed like the Chinese do in Hong Kong, and he only used the crook arm to feed himself and to gaff fish with. He had a big shark hook with the barb filed off that he used to strap to the stump. Of course John had got Worker's Compensation for his arm after the accident. Arch asked him once how much he had got but he didn't know. He reckoned it must have been a fair cheque because it took him and his mates three weeks to drink it out.

Mulletgut Olaf came from one of them squarehead countries where they can't say "J" but they use it a lot in their spelling to confuse outsiders. One of his cousins had come to Australia on a wool clipper once and took home a case of Bundaberg rum, with which he made something of a reputation for himself in his home district. Even the Aurora Borealis was lit up better that year, they reckon. Olaf had got a bottle for himself, and after drinking it reckoned he'd found the answer to his prayers, so he shipped out on the next available ship to live near the place where they made it. He was a short barrel-chested bloke with skinny legs. He said he got that build from rowing boats round the fjords.

Well, these two welcomed Arch, first because they liked him and second because he brought three bottles of rum with him. They opened a bottle straight away to give them strength to go and pump yabbies for bait, so they could go fishing that night. When the bottle was empty they went and pumped for the yabbies and got lots of them, big muscular ones full of fight. There was one big one in particular, with a green stripe round his fighting claw, that all the others seemed a bit windy of. This big one sat in a corner of the bait box and scowled, while the others argued and fought all over the rest of the box and didn't get too close to him.

"Yee whiz, Yonny, dot vun mus' be Irish yabby," said Olaf. "Look at dem udders yompin' avay von him."

"Ah, shut yer gob, ye eel eatin' wreck," said Johnny.

Arch says Olaf used to like eels to eat, and he used to catch them and skin them and smoke them in an old tank till they looked like surcingles, and Johnny couldn't stand the sight of them.

Well, they covered the yabbies in salt water and put them away for the afternoon, and then they all laid down under some sea oaks and cracked the second bottle. Then they had a feed of black duck baked in clay and waited for sundown. Arch says he must have gone to sleep or something about then because the next thing he knew it was dark and the hurricane lamp was alight and the other two were shaking him awake to find where he'd planted the third bottle. Arch says that he'd been too cunning to leave it where they'd find it easy in case they might drop it and break it or something.

At any rate, the three of them collected the bottle and the yabbies and their gear and piled it into Johnny's old dinghy, and Johnny sculled down to a channel he knew near the bar. Then they dropped the pick and had a drink and caught a yabby each out of the bait box, and chucked their lines into the water. They caught a few whiting and pulled in four big Queensland blue mudcrabs with claws like multigrips that they brought inboard with the landing net and then left to scuttle round the bottom of the boat. Arch objected to this a bit but Olaf said, "If you didn't moof dey vood dink your veet vos a sdone," so Arch sat there growling and very carefully not moofing his veet.

Johnny said then that they had better shift to the deep hole just inside the bar and try there. He said that there was either not enough wind, or too much or something. So Olaf pulled up the pick and they sculled to a place about a hundred yards off the bank and anchored again. Then they all had another drink, and Olaf caught two of them little knot eels that tie knots in themselves and pitched them into the bottom of the boat in spite of Johnny's going crook. The two eels quietly tied their tails together in a reef knot and went to sleep. Then Johnny caught a ten pound wire netting cod and Arch pulled in a four-and-a-half pound flathead and knocked the bottle of rum over so about a pint spilt into the inch of bilgewater that was slopping around in the bottom of the boat.

The other two couldn't say too much about this accident because, after all, it was his rum. Johnny did mention that his grandfather was a hamfisted elbow-fingered stumblebum, and that Arch reminded him of him, but that was all. Then Olaf got this terrific bite on the big line he had hung over the side.

"Gum here," he said. "Gum do Poppa. Ach yeesus, Yonny, sdop yerkin' de boat!"

Then before they could stop him he pulled a four foot conger eel, all snapping jaws and slimy threshing coils, into the mass of lines, yabbies, mudcrabs, cod, flathead, whiting, rum, and bare feet that covered the bottom of the dinghy. The hurricane lamp fell over and went out. Johnny took a header over the side, followed by Arch. They both reckoned they weren't fit enough to rassle that slippery creature in the dark. Olaf was more optimistic for about ten seconds but then even he left. They swam miserably ashore and sat on the bank until morning in their wet clothes. Word got round among the mozzies and sandflies that there were three human bar-rooms stranded nearby in the mangroves; so they were all pretty near sober and bloodless by the time the sun poked a bloodshot eye up over the eastern horizon. Johnny abused Olaf all night, but Olaf was happy.

"Pluddy beaut, dot eel. Like the pluddy Midgard Serpent, yet," he said once.

They swam out to the dinghy and peered over the gunwale. They were delighted to find that everything was under control, though all the rum and bilgewater was gone, drunk by the boat's inhabitants.

The big conger eel had passed out. It was stretched full length on the bottom boards with its head pillowed on the coil of anchor rope. The cod was telling the flathead it loved it. The four mudcrabs were neatly tied up and helpless; apparently they had got nasty and started to pick on the knot eels who quietly tied them up then went to sleep with their tails hitched together in a double sheet bend. But it was the big yabby that really surprised them, said Arch. He'd made all the other yabbies untangle their lines and roll them up neatly on their proper reels. He saluted them gravely as they scrambled over the side, then collapsed snoring in the bilges, dead to the world. Johnny was speechless for once. He just pulled in the pick and started sculling for home.

Arch asked me to write it all down so if any of you blokes ever pump a whopping big yabby with a green stripe round his claw, don't use him for bait, will you? Just put him back in his hole on the mudflat and apologise.

The Crafty Barramundi

My Uncle Arch went up to the Gulf Country once in the days before there were any beef roads or road trains. Things are pretty willing up there now, but nothing to what they were when he was young, says Arch. There were none of these beer cans in those days. Publicans didn't buy too much beer because the heat used to make the bottles explode. They used to buy rum, mostly, because the blokes like to feel the results when they had a drink, and with rum you could start to feel the results nearly straightaway sometimes. Rum was used to cure infections, cauterise spear wounds, treat fever and even as a mosquito net. In fact when I heard him once talking about a Burketown mosquito net and asked him what it was, he told me that if you drank a bottle of OP rum, then the mosquitoes had a job to worry you, and they certainly wouldn't wake you up. In fact, your mates would have a job the next morning. Gulf Country rum was great stuff. You could use it to start a fire with wet wood, or fill your cigarette lighter, or anything. One bloke was even foolish enough to pour some into the petrol tank of his motor car one day when he ran out of juice ten miles from the garage. They never saw the car again after that, Arch says. The last they saw of it it was chasing a bulldozer and offering to fight it.

But that's beside the point. The point is that he brought the bullock wagon with its load of stores into Jackandandy homestead and off-loaded there. It was only halfway through the dry season, so he had plenty of time to get back with the load of hides he had for back-loading; so he decided to camp there for a week and give his beasts a chance to line their rib cages with decent grass before they took off back down-country. While the plant were filling their bellies, him and Mick the Skinner started in loading the salted hides onto the wagon. It was a terrible job, because of the way the hides stank. It didn't help any that Mick hadn't had a bath since the midwife had finished with him. He used to stroll around in the middle of a little swarm of blowflies, but none of them landed on him because if they got within six inches of his skin they used to pass out from asphyxiation before they could lower their undercarriage ready to land. Mostly they just sort of used to hang round him hopefully like a mob of sinners round the Pearly Gates. They could see the fun going on inside, and even hear the music, but they knew they couldn't get to their Promised Land. Must have been tantalising for them, but there you are.

At any rate, Arch and Mick the Skinner were piling the last of the hides on top of the load for a jockey when one of the Aboriginal stockmen came riding in to the homestead, and went and asked the Boss for a handful of dynamite and a detonator. Of course the Boss wanted to know why; and it turned out that there was a great big barramundi in the lagoon where the musterers were camped, and they had tried every way they knew to catch the big fish with lines and traps, but it only laughed at their efforts. They reckoned that the only way they'd be able to get their backscratchers onto it would be blow out the rock bar at the end of the pool and let the water drain away; then they could get in and round it up with their stockwhips.

The Boss had been to school once, and he remembered that there was something about how it wasn't sportsmanlike to blow up a fish's home just so you could get at it and cut slabs off it to sink your laughing gear into, or so he said. Then too, that hole was the best standing waterhole on the whole run, and he didn't want it ruined. So he wouldn't give the blokes any dynamite.

He said that they would have to catch it fairly and in a sportsmanlike manner. Then he said he'd go back with the stockman and have a go at the fish himself. When Arch and Mick the Skinner heard this, they both wanted to go too; and the Boss said they could so long as Mick camped half-a-mile away downwind from the rest of them.

So they got a coil of Manila rope from the store, and a couple of the big hooks that they used to hang up the dressed bullocks after they'd been butchered, then they took off for the waterhole, the Boss in the sulky with the gear, and the stockman and Mick following along. Arch came last with a couple of his best bullocks because he thought he might find a use for them, and sure enough he did. I'll tell you about that in a minute.

Well, to cut a long story short, a week later they were all very frustrated and vexed with each other, but most of all with the barramundi. It could snap Manila rope like bits of cotton, and as for meat-hooks, it used to straighten them out then tie them into true lover's knots and throw them back on the bank. Then it used to stick its head out of the water out of reach of their stockwhips, and laugh at them. The Boss was thinking of going back to the homestead for some Old Man Nobel's bait, and to hell with sportsmanship when Arch had an idea.

Now, Arch hadn't been taking much part in the fishing business. It seemed to him that it would take some pretty unorthodox sort of handling to land this big fish; so he sat on top of a nearby hill upwind and thought about things while his bullocks grazed on the feed around the base. Actually, he didn't feel any real animosity toward the water dweller, for it had done him no harm and anyway he wasn't all that fond of fish as tucker. A decent bit of corned beef with some damper and boiled pumpkin washed down with a strong tea was more the kind of feed he preferred. He said it stuck to your ribs better, and you didn't have to keep rushing off for more all the time. That's true, too. I know because he once cooked a feed for me; but that's beside the point. The point is that one night, just when the anglers were getting desperate, the barramundi came up to where Arch's bullocks were having a drink of water from the rock bar and said a lot of sneering things about Arch, like why wasn't he game to have a go at it, and he was a piker, and things like that. The bullocks didn't answer, it was beneath their dignity; but when they got back to camp they told Arch about it. That was that. From then on the fish's fate was sealed, though it didn't know it.

Arch remembered that his mate old Black Peter had once told him about a vine that grew in the scrub near Cairns. If you pounded it to a pulp in water and then tipped the water into a billabong then all the fish got sort of punch-drunk and often came right out of the water and beat one another up on the reed-beds, thus enabling the Aborigines to get a decent feed without too much trouble. When they'd got enough they'd throw the rest back so there'd be more the next time they came that way. Arch knew it would work here, too. The snag was that there wasn't any scrub around for hundreds of miles to go and get the right kind of vine; and it had to be the right one or it wouldn't work. He was still thinking about it when he went down to get his tea with the others. The Boss was talking some nonsense about blokes who went fishing with flies or something, and one of the ringers said they must be relatives of Mick the Skinner because he did too, and everybody laughed except Mick, who got sulky. But when Arch finished laughing, suddenly he got an idea. He called the Boss off to one side and explained the plan to him, and the Boss said it ought to work. Then they both rolled up in their blueys and wouldn't tell the others what they were laughing about, which irritated the ringers no end, because they were a fun-loving lot.

Early next morning Arch fitted both the bullocks with yokes and chains while the ringers watched in amazement. Even the barramundi stuck its head out of the water and watched. Arch led one bullock to one end of the billabong and the other one to the other. Then he nodded to the Boss and the Boss yelled; "Lassoo Mick and tie him up!" No sooner said than done, and Mick was soon tied up on the ground. Arch took one end of the rope and hitched it to one of the bullocks, while the Boss took the other and did the same to the other one. Then they walked the bullocks away from the waterhole and Mick got gradually towed in. He didn't want to go, mind you, but he went! When he was in mid-water the Boss walked his bullock away and Arch backed his up until Mick was towed to the Boss's end of the water, then they reversed and towed him the other way, and so on. Pretty soon all sorts of things started to come out of the waterhole and walk away downstream. A saltwater crocodile came out and was sick on the bank and a whole tribe of crayfish came out with one claw holding their noses and the other waving feebly in the air. Turtles, saw-fish, shrimps, bony herrings and all sorts of other fish came along too, followed by hundreds of eels. One by one they crossed the rock bar and headed out of sight round the bend toward the next hole. Even the water seemed to be trying to climb over the bar, but of course it couldn't. Last of all the barramundi appeared. Its face was blue from holding its breath, but it couldn't last any longer.

"Do you give in?" yelled the Boss when he saw it. The poor fish groaned and nodded. "Righto, so long as you know we've won. You better stop being so cheeky, or we'll bring him back again," threatened the Boss. The fish crossed its heart and spat.

Well, they dragged Mick to the bank and stood him on his head till he finished draining. He'd stopped yelling by this time and could only wheeze. The ringers gathered round and looked him over.

"Well, what do you know!" said one of the Aboriginal ringers. "He's not one of us after all. Hasn't he got thin, too!"

Well, they peeled lots of old clothes off Mick as though he was an onion, until at last he stood there looking like a sapling with the bark peeled off. His heels were bigger than his buttocks. The Boss gave him a shirt and trousers, but really he was never the same afterwards, and he left the Gulf country soon after and was never seen again. Arch came safely back south. If you go up that way, though, don't be surprised if a lot of blowflies come and sit on you. They're still trying to find Mick and they don't know where he's gone.

The Cunning Cockroach

My Uncle Arch was working as supercargo on an old copra lugger once, round the Fly Coast in New Guinea, and he reckons that if ever a place was well-named it was that one. Sandflies and mozzies in millions. What they used to do was to sail along the beach from village to village picking up any copra the natives had ready and then taking it along to Daru where they unloaded it into little steamers for Moresby. There was only Arch and the Skipper that were a bit pale, the rest of the mob on board were all shades and shapes, and a pretty rough mob. They used to drink rum and spit over the side. That's all they had to do for recreation, Arch reckons.

Arch and the skipper lived in a sort of tin-roofed, tin-walled box right aft. The crew slept where they fell over, usually. It wasn't much tropical romance, what with the copra bugs and the mozzies and sandflies and the fact that the skipper and crew only had a wash when they got caught out in the rain. Fortunately, this was pretty frequent, the weather being what it was up there. Arch reckons that once they came to Brisbane and tied up at Pinkenba, the fertiliser works got up in the night and moved a quarter of a mile inland to get away from the pong.

As I said, they didn't have much recreation on board until one day Arch found the skipper staring over the rails and thinking. He reckons the skipper didn't do this very often, so he noticed it in particular. It seemed that the skipper was trying to work out some way to run races on board so they could have a bet if they felt like it, but he hadn't been able to work out any method. They couldn't swim because, although there were no sharks, it was only because the crocodiles frightened them away.

Well, I don't know if you have noticed, but Arch has a pretty fertile mind, and once he sets his mind to a problem he usually solves it. The solution to this problem didn't baffle him for long. He worked out that if you drew a circle in chalk on the deck, and then a tiny circle in the middle of the big one, you could start up to four cockroaches in the central circle, and then the first one who crossed the outer circle would be the winner. After a few weeks they had it down to a fine art. Runners were kept in empty matchboxes. When the race was about to start the trainers would put the matchbox upside down on the deck in the starters' circle. Then they would slowly and carefully slide the tray out. They would sit and tap on the bottom of the tray to persuade the cockroaches not to hang upside down on the roof of the box. Then the word would be given and the boxes would all be lifted at the one time and the cockies would be away. It was very thrilling because sometimes a real good goer would race straight for the finish, baulk, and then run like hell back to the starting circle and jib and refuse to move any more. It was the closest to being a fair race that was ever invented in the world.

Of course there was trouble sometimes. A big ex-headhunter once lost his balance for a minute and stepped on the current champion that was owned by a slightly reformed Kukukuku and both reverted to their uncivilised state and had to be stopped by the skipper with an empty rum bottle. What with the high mortality rate among the runners the ship was soon cleaner than it had been for years. You'd find blokes sneaking round in the middle of the night trying to catch fresh runners. Every three weeks they'd have to declare a closed season to let the harried survivors breed up again. It was a great sport.

Arch said that what none of them had given much attention to was the Law of the Survival of the Fittest. According to Darwin the fittest survive, and this was the case on the lugger. What happened was that at the end of six months there was what can only be described as a race of super cockroaches on board. They ran to length of leg rather than stoutness, and they had a getaway that Roger Bannister would have envied. Real toey, Arch reckoned. Of course, when you did manage to catch one you had a real goer, and as the sport had caught on in Daru and in the villages along the coast, the boys found they could really make a lot of money. When you went ashore all you'd see would be a circle drawn somewhere surrounded by a lot of big backsides stuck up into the air as they cheered on their favourites. The boys from the lugger used to clean up the betting with the superior breed that had been developed on board.

Arch had pretty well given up racing them, when one night he was lying on his bunk working on an idea he had for slinging the cabin of the ship in gimbals so it would stay still in the roughest weather. There was a sort of flash on the outer edge of his field of vision and he realised that what he had seen was the fastest thing in the animal kingdom outside the dingbat, that rare creature of the Central Australian desert.

The cockroach Arch was looking at was a long slim creature with powerful shoulders and magnificent loins. It held its head proudly, and it had the gleam of intelligence in its beady eyes, like the pony ridden by the Man from Snowy River. Arch could see at a glance that this was the sure winner for best of breed in any cockroach show in the world. He knew that if he could only get his hands on it and bring it to racing pitch he'd clean up a fortune; even against the kind of competition that was around by then. So he started very slowly to move his right hand round in a sort of panzer movement from the rear. The cockroach waited until he made his grab and then dodged him with great ease, displaying some of the fanciest footwork Arch had ever seen. It ducked into a crack between two planks where it watched him, waving its feelers in the air. Arch could see that strategy was needed so he made his preparations.

First he got a tin of molasses and mixed it with Overproof rum. He spread this on a bit of paper on the messdeck table, and went to bed. The roach came out of the crack and started to bog into the molasses. Another more muscular thickset roach came along but the racer had a skinful of the OP by this time and it got stuck into the big one and easily drove it away though it was giving away at least half-an-ounce weight. After another half-hour it was so full and bogged down in the treacle that it passed out, and Arch swears he heard it singing. He carefully retrieved it and put it in an old kerosene tin to sleep off its excesses.

The next morning the roach was sober again and resigned to its captivity, though it had an awful hangover. Arch gave it a bit of aspro to chew on, then a drink of warm rum and milk for a hair of the dog. Its gratitude was pathetic, and a warm love and understanding was born between man and roach at that time. They had a toothbrush on board that a missionary had left once, and Arch used it to groom the cockroach until its carapace was gleaming and it was rearing to go.

He cleaned up all opposition along the coast, of course. Nothing put into the ring could compete with Cocky, as he named it. By the time they got back to Daru he had chalked up an unbroken series of wins unequalled in the history of the sport and Arch knew he had world-class material on his hands. But when they tied up to the wharf at Daru this big Torres Strait Islander came on board with a challenge. Reckoned he had a beast that'd knock Cocky hollow. Arch had every confidence in his little friend so he backed him with all his winnings and the back pay the skipper owed him. The arrangements were that the races were to be the best of three, with a field of two only, match races they called them. The local publican held the stakes and there was a big turnout to see the championship of the Coral Sea run-off. The races took place in the local bar, which was also the courthouse and church when not in use as a pub. Daru's a funny place, or at least it was then.

There were a number of preliminary events run by less skilled cockroaches and so excitement was at fever pitch by the time for the main event. One bloke slipped a disc and had to watch the rest of the races laid out on a table. Another bloke was disqualified for blowing on his opponent's roach. There was a dogfight outside. Things were pretty lively that night. Then Arch and the T.I. bloke fronted up with their champions, and the main event started.

Cocky was in beautiful condition, and there was a roar of admiration went up when Arch was grooming him with the toothbrush. But consternation reigned when the other bloke produced his champion. It was a huge slippery-looking muscular roach with shifty eyes, rather ragged-looking but obviously in the pink of condition and raring to go. The first race was a walkover for Cocky, who strode out in fine style and was safe in his matchbox before the big bloke reached the finish. After five minutes' spell they went at it again. This time the big one deliberately tripped Cocky before racing for the line, and thus won by taking an unfair advantage. Cocky's backers protested but the ref. reckoned that there wasn't anything in the rules about tripping and so they were even at the end of the second and the final had to be run to decide the winner.

Well, the word was given and they sprinted off. They ran side by side and neck and neck for the line. The big bloke was really running this time but Cocky was holding him off. Then, just before they crossed the finish, the big roach deliberately leapt into the air and came down on Cocky's back. Cocky raced gamely on and crossed the line a fraction ahead but he collapsed. He died that night, and the world seemed an emptier place to Arch for his going. Of course he won the money, but money isn't everything in this world. He donged the big bloke for unfair tactics, but he never caught the villainous roach, who disappeared safely into the woodwork. That's why Arch gave up the job and came back to Australia, and why the roaches in Daru are the speediest and strongest in the world to this day.

Treacle Jimmy

My Uncle Arch went prospecting with this bloke who was called Treacle Jimmy because that's what he liked to eat most on his damper. I mean, most blokes eat golden syrup, but Jimmy reckoned that syrup didn't have the body to it that treacle had, so he used to buy it by the forty-four gallon drum so's he wouldn't run out. Arch didn't mind. He was never what you'd call a fussy eater, like these young blokes you see nowadays that blow the ashes off their damper before they bite into it. A bit of charcoal's good for the teeth and bowels. I mean, you've only got to look at pigs. They eat charcoal, and you've never heard of a pig with indigestion, have you?

Anyway, Arch went prospecting with this bloke called Treacle Jimmy out from Emu Park and Yeppoon. That's a funny bit of country, if you like. There's copper and lead and gold, but though it's got a couple of declared fields, they cut out years ago, and all that's left is a bit of metal in little pockets here and there. They didn't do too well, what with one thing and another, and the mosquitoes were thick, and the flies were bad enough to swear at, so they weren't too fat or comfortable. They used to go into town once a fortnight for a bit of flour and fat and a few snorts of rum. For the rest they lived off the land, such as it was. Any of you that's used a crab-hook, or run a gill net, or rigged a deadfall for wallabies will know what I mean. Their main expense was the rum, of course. And this big drum of treacle every now and then.

Well, they decided that if they were going to be able to get a snort of rum occasionally they'd better make some arrangements. They went to the local dump and came up with some old copper pipe and a couple of four-gallon drums and they started to put through a batch of moonshine every now and then. It was real good stuff, and very economical too, as long as you didn't spill too much around. It'd lift varnish and polish metal. It'd start a rusted bolt or fill your cigarette lighter or whatever you wanted. It'd even take grease stains out of cloth, but you had to be careful or it'd take the cloth as well.

They never really noticed the flies and mosquitoes after they started distilling this stuff. Any mosquito that bit them used to go straight off and challenge a bull ant. Things were pretty comfortable, in fact. If they could only have found the reef they were looking for their cup of happiness would have runneth over. As it was, they had tracked the gold up a gully to near where they had the still planted when they got their troubles.

Their troubles really began when the old nanny goat got into their scranbag while they were out scratching and ate all their flour and tobacco. I mean, you can do without flour at a pinch if you've got beef, but no tobacco means that you don't get your vitamins, and you're likely to get scurvy and Barcoo Rot and other things too dreadful to mention. And of course they had no money, because they'd just been to town and blued it on food and tobacco, for the benefit of the goat. Not that the goat didn't benefit, she did. She looked remarkably fit and healthy. But if you're used to a smoke after tea while you drink your pannikin of home made rum you miss it. So Treacle Jimmy decided that they just had to get some money from somewhere and he decided that he'd sell a gallon or two of the moonshine rum for cash.

He tucked a couple of dozen bottles under his arm and headed for the little fishing place down on the coast of Keppel Bay where the prawnie boats dock. He had no difficulty in trading. He came home with six two-ounce plugs, a bag of flour, and four pounds of king prawns.

This was the beginning of that period in Arch's life he sometimes calls *la dolce vita*. Him and Jimmy used to just sit round stoking up the fire now and then and running another batch, and smoking plug tobacco and eating damper and king prawns and wallaby and drinking rum and goat's milk. It was too good to last. Arch reckons.

What happened was that a little prawnie bloke called Venial Sin got full on their product and went to Emu Park to get a few hanks of twine to mend his nets. He was so full of *joie de vivre* that he cleaned up two pineapple farmers, a real estate salesman, three tourists, and the engine crew of a goods train. This all happened before they closed the branch line there. At any rate there was a company of commandos training there and they came and took turns at sitting on him until he faded out, and they saved him until he came to so they could find out where he was getting it from. Venial Sin was only a little quiet bloke when he was sober, especially when he had a real hangover, and blow me if he didn't spill the beans. The officer in charge of these commandos had no sense of humour and he reported to the police in Rockhampton about it.

The police didn't want to do too much about it. Country policemen are pretty live and let live sort of blokes, I've found. Really, they hadn't minded so much that the prawnie blokes hadn't been coming to town quite so frequently, because the prawnie-boat blokes were no team of marching girls, and life had been easier for the police when they didn't have to play "Waltz me around again, Willie" every Saturday night with a hairy, hard team of blokes who thought stoush was fun and who smelled like old seaboot socks because they rarely bathed. But, once a complaint had been made and they couldn't talk this officer bloke out of it, they decided they'd have to go through the motions. Especially as there was a new young Customs bloke in town and he was one of those everything-by-the-book sort of blokes and he insisted on going along.

"An illicit still contravenes Section two. Para. 3(c) P. Sergeant, and I feel it is my duty," said the Customs bloke.

So they got into the Land Rover and away down to the prawnies' settlement. Of course, nobody had ever heard of two blokes who sold rum at seven and six a gallon. Venial Sin had been sent to the South, to get him out of the road, and there were no witnesses beyond the bad breath of the inhabitants. But the Sergeant was a shrewdie, and he took to the hills with the Constable and the Customs man. They stumbled over the track that led to where Arch and Treacle Jimmy had their diggings.

Now the prawnies had given them plenty of warning, so everything was hidden away when they finally got wind of the police coming. The old nanny goat took to the top of the nearest crag and stayed there sneering all the time the outsiders were in the camp. They searched, of course, but they didn't find anything. Arch and Jimmy were too cunning for them. But while they were there there was one drawback, they had to work, so they had started in sinking on the shaft they'd been working on before they found that distilling paid better than prospecting.

So there was Arch down the drive and Jimmy swinging on the windlass when the official party came into the camp. The Customs bloke was all official, and said whereas and heretofore and things like that, but the Sergeant put the billy on and made tea and in his gentle and roundabout fashion let the two prospectors know they'd better stick to producing for home consumption and not for export, all without mentioning the fact that he knew they had a still at all. Arch and Jimmy liked the Sergeant, he knew what the score was so they appreciated him. When he'd gone they sat on their logs near the fire and looked at each other.

"Well, that's the end of it then," said Jimmy.

Arch suggested that they get a real big herd of nanny goats and feed them on their product and sell the resulting rum and milk. But Treacle Jimmy was a realist.

"Look," he said, "that little skinny weed'd only find some subsection in 'is blasted Act that'd scupper us. It's no use, mate, we're beggared."

And he pulled a big stone out of the ground from near where he was sitting and went to throw it after the police. But Arch's eyes stuck out like raisins in a duff, and he caught Jimmy's wrist. The gold was fair hanging out of that rock in knobs! They'd been camped fair on the cap of the outcrop all the time.

Well, they sold out for a large sum of money, and went south to Brisbane after that, and that was the time that Arch nearly got married but I'll tell you about that another time. In the meantime, if you run into a bloke that lives mainly on treacle on his damper instead of syrup, you can ask him if this story isn't true. He'll tell you.

The Deadly Quicksand

Shortly after my Uncle Arch and his mate Treacle Jimmy found the gold near Yeppoon and went to Brisbane for a spree, they were broke again. This was mainly due to Arch nearly getting married, but I'll tell you about that another time. The main thing was that they had to get out of Brisbane after what Jimmy did to the visiting opera singer. Not that the opera singer minded but you know what newspapers are. They rolled their blueys and filled their nosebags and jumped the rattler out of Roma Street goods yards, and wound up in Longreach. From there they went west toward the Territory border, to look for opals, Arch says. Things were more uncivilised out there in those days than they are even now. They didn't stay long in town, just long enough to get some tucker and buy a bottle of rum so they would get their vitamins. Then they headed for the sunset, on foot of course.

About a week out of town they came to this creek where there was a bit of water left, and as it was promising-looking country they decided to camp there for a while and look the place over. It was average country for the place and the time of year; nearly dead flat except for some sandstone hills; no trees much except some scrubby thorny bush growing along the creek and ghost gums and an occasional patch of gidgee. There were plenty of roos around, so they had no trouble about fresh meat. They didn't have a gun so Arch used to just run them down on foot and then trip them up so they fell and broke their necks. He was in such good nick after Brisbane that he even used to trip them up after heading them right into camp so he didn't have to carry them home after he'd caught them.

One night they had a visitor. He was an Aboriginal stockman who was out doing a bit of boundary riding. They had to be hospitable so they finished up the bottle of rum at a sitting instead of making it last as long as they had intended. This left them in a bit of a pickle as far as getting their vitamins was concerned. It was Jimmy who solved the difficulty, the way he did the other time. Snag was they didn't have any equipment to build a still, and there wasn't a dump for miles to go for materials.

They hollowed out a section of old log so it would hold about six gallons. Then they lined it with clay. They didn't have much in the way of stuff to work with for ingredients, either, but Jimmy found a place one day where some droving plant must have camped and thrown away the guts of a Queensland blue pumpkin. This had grown into pumpkin vines and there were a lot of pumpkins ready for harvesting. They cut up a few of these and put them in the hollow in the log, then they put in about six pounds of quandongs, a few lumps out of the sugar bag, and a tin of mouldy apricot jam. Then they topped her up with creek water and waited for the brew to work. A couple of days later she was really working, and a week later the bubbling had stopped. They were peering cautiously at it when the same Aboriginal stockman rode up with his dogs.

"What you blokes doin'?" he asked.

They explained that they felt the need for a bit of refreshment and had been doing a bit of home brewing. Now they were doubtful about it and weren't too anxious about trying it out. This stockman was a pretty shrewd bloke so he suggested that they try it out on one of his dogs that'd been a bit off-colour for the past three days.

"C'mere, Achilles," he roared, and the dog came up.

They caught it and poured about half-a-glass down its throat. Then they let it go and watched.

The dog seemed a bit bewildered at first, but a couple of seconds later it roared once and took off across the plains like a streak. It was out of sight in a second. Before anybody could say anything it was back, driving a medium-size bunyip in front of it, heeling it at every jump. They vanished in the direction of Mount Isa and were never seen again. The stockman looked thoughtful.

"Seems to be all right," he said.

So he carefully sipped a little, rolled it round his tongue, and swallowed. He said it was an adequate if rough vintage with an amusing bouquet of quandong.

So they strained it off through Arch's spare flannel and bottled it in blue castor oil bottles that they found near the old drovers' camp. Drovers were great believers in castor oil, and so they needed to be with all the sand they swallowed tailing the mob. They needed constant lubrication for their gritty bowels. Things were pretty tough outback in those days.

The stockman said there still seemed to be something missing, so he added a full packet of APC powders he had in his swag in case he got bitten by a snake. This really improved the flavour out of sight, but it was still too strong to drink straight, so Arch took the billy down to the creek to get a drop of water to break it down a bit.

The stockman said he was in no hurry so he unrolled his swag and said he'd camp with them for a day or so and build up his reserve of vitamins.

When Arch got down to the creek he found the water was muddy from where the dog had crossed at full gallop with the bunyip, so he went upstream a bit to a place where he'd never got water before and waded out to midstream to fill the billy. Next thing he knew the stockman came charging flat out through the bushes shouting to him to look out for the quicksand but by then it was too late. The treacherous sand had him, and try as he might he couldn't get his feet free.

Now this quicksand had been there for a long time and it really enjoyed sucking things down into its depths, so it was prepared to take its time with Arch. He struggled a bit but he couldn't get his feet out. The quicksand grinned to itself and pulled all the nails out of his boots and swallowed them. Arch tried to get away again. The quicksand pulled the soles off his boots and sucked them down.

Jimmy and the stockman tied their belts together and threw the end to Arch. They both pulled. The quicksand only laughed and sucked the dye out of the socks Arch happened to be wearing. Arch could see it was no go. He was really stuck this time, and it was beginning to look as though his seamy career was coming to an end. He struggled a bit more. The quicksand began to tug at the cuffs of his pants. Arch tightened his belt and hung onto the tops of his trousers as hard as he could but it was no go. He did manage to get his watch and knife out of their pouches as the trousers slipped under, but that was all.

"Well, hooray, Jimmy. You can have me swag. Here, mate, you can have me watch an' knife. Can I have a last drink?"

Jimmy said, "It ain't going to be much use to you where you're going. Still, we been mates a long time so

I suppose you can have a drink, even if you don't live to enjoy it."

"You won't need us to mix it for yer, either," said the stockman. "You can just open yer mouth shortly an' the water'll run in."

Jimmy went back to the camp and came back with a bottle each. The quicksand pulled a bit harder. It was above Arch's knees by now, and really enjoying itself.

"Thanks for the watch an' knife, mate," said the stockman. "Would yer mind tossin' the end of me belt back? It cost me fifteen bob an' I'd hate ter lose it."

"All right," said Arch.

Just then Jimmy came back with the bottles and gave one to the stockman, and tossed one to Arch. He was a crook shot, and though Arch reached for it fell short, and the quicksand sucked it under.

"You clumsy beggar," roared Arch. "Now it's wasted!"

"Well, you can go ter blazes if yer think I'm goin' ter waste another bottle on such a clumsy bearded black b ..."

Jimmy was cut off in mid-sentence by the quicksand. It still hung onto Arch, but not as hard. It started to heave and bubble. The water got a boiling disturbed look about it. The sand started to go a pale shade of green.

Well, you know yourself how it is when you're pretty full and somebody talks you into that one for the road. You know you shouldn't have it but you do. Jimmy's brew was the last thing as far as the quicksand was concerned. After all, it was already trying to deal with Arch's trousers, not to mention his socks. It started to erupt, to put it politely.

First it chucked Arch up onto the bank. Then it chucked his socks and boots and trousers after him. Then it sort of settled for a minute, but it was getting greener all the time.

"I think we'd better shift," said the stockman anxiously.

They took shelter behind a gum and peered cautiously at the quicksand. The quicksand seemed to swell up. It turned pale. Then it threw out seven hundred and thirty-six steers, a hundred and twenty-one Aborigines, four stockhorses, three dingoes, a packsaddle, a quartpot, a box of matches, and a little hairy prospector who had got caught on his way to the Hall's Creek rush.

Well, Arch dried his trousers on a bush and they all had a drink and watched the quicksand. Presently they saw it get shakily up and move off down the creek in the direction of Lake Eyre. The little hairy bloke stayed with Arch and Jimmy after all the grog got drunk but the stockman went off in a huff after Arch made him give the watch and pocket-knife back. Arch and Jimmy

and the little hairy bloke, whose name was Knuckles
O'Hara, went partners after that for a while until Arch
left them to go back to his old job bullock driving up on
the Atherton Tableland.

The Betoota Rum Festival

My Uncle Arch was out Betoota way once a fair while ago. This was in the days when everybody still wore whiskers and smoked plug tobacco. You really had to be fit to smoke that tobacco. If you did the drawback your mouth looked and felt like an old bit of dried leather. The only thing they drank was rum, and they usually made it themselves. They used to try it on a bullock first, and if the bullock lived they reckoned it was safe. Just before the beginning of shearing when everybody was broke and couldn't afford expensive imported rum they'd all be brewing their own, and the country would be full of bullocks either stone blind staggering molo or else standing round the billabongs drinking water and suffering from dreadful hangovers.

At any rate, the time I'm talking about, there was a mob of about forty shearers camped round the place waiting for sheds. They were all broke to the wide and their skins were cracking for a drink. This happened every year. The only asset in the whole mob was a gold medal one bloke had; he'd won it in a buck-hauling contest at Santiago — the one in South America, not the station in New South Wales. He used to go there to load ships with bird manure, said Arch, though what would be the use of a ship-load of bird manure he didn't speculate about. As for buck-hauling, I'll tell you about that another time. For the present, it's enough to know that this bloke had the gold medal, and he was very proud of it and wouldn't part with it. They might have taken it off him and tried to spend it only the local shanty was dry, too. Everything was dry that year. They'd even run out of ingredients for their own brew of rum, and all the bullocks looked much better for it. But that's beside the point.

The point is that Arch had a real brainwave about how they could get a free supply of grog for the following year when the same dry time came round. There was a bloke in the mob that had been a forger in England. In fact, that was the reason he happened to be in Australia. Arch got him and another old lag who used to make dud two-bobs for a sideline, and they went into a huddle. Next day or so they were pretty busy, and then Arch called the mob round by belting on the bottom of a tin dish with an iron spoon and explained what they were going to do.

The forger had carved some blocks of mulga wood and printed a real impressive letterhead with boot polish. He was supposed to mix it with metho, but he drank the metho instead. He would have drunk the polish too, but Arch was watching. At any rate, him and Arch wrote this letter to all the rum-makers whose addresses they could get off the labels of the empty bottles around the billabong where they were camped. The letter said that a great rum festival would be held annually at the billabong, and the prize was a gold medal. Round about here the champion buck-hauler started to protest but the mob sat on him before he could get started. Jimmy One-leg didn't think much of the idea, but he was always jealous of Arch, so nobody took any notice of him. They were all a bit doubtful, as a matter of fact, but they reckoned it was worth a try. So they posted the letters off, took the medal and gave it to the forger, and elected a committee of three very fast runners to watch him, *and* each other, while he made a Champion Rum medal out of it. Then they gave it to the local policeman to look after, and forgot about the whole thing.

Until the next year, when the rum started to arrive. There were three bullock drays of it, besides a load brought in by a donkey team and one by an Afghan with his camels. Jimmy One-leg didn't have a word to say, but all the other blokes cheered Arch. Then Jimmy said — real nasty — "Who gets the medal?"

Arch thought for a while, then he said, "Who sent most rum?"

And that's how a great big fellow in the island of Trinidad came to get this buck-hauling medal, but he couldn't read so it didn't matter. Every year they still hold the festival, though Arch hasn't been to one for a long time. Every year they sell just enough of the entries to buy another gold medal, and drink the rest.

So now you know the true story. Of course the idea caught on all over the world, and wherever you get a thirsty mob of layabouts that want to fill up on free grog you get these festivals. They have wine festivals in South Australia and Victoria, and France and Yugoslavia, and they have beer festivals at Prague and Munich. Even the Sydney Show and the Brisbane Exhibition have woken up to the lurk. There's three or four blokes out front taking sips and spitting them in a box of sawdust while the rest of the mob are round the back getting stuck into it. That's what Arch says, and he ought to know. After all, he started it, long ago, out at the billabong near Betoota.

Arch still drinks rum, but not as much as he used to do. He says it spoils the wind, and interferes with buck-hauling. He ought to know.

The Great Sheepdog Trials

My Uncle Arch had a sheepdog called Charles once, and it was the smartest sheepdog between Melbourne and wherever Arch happened to be at the time. It could read brands on horses. It was entirely trustworthy too. Most of the time they weren't working Arch used to let Charles look after their money. This saved him having to worry about paying bus conductors but it was sometimes awkward when they were on a railway station and he needed a penny in a hurry. Charles never needed a penny. In fact Arch made this plain to me one day when we were talking. I said to him, "I expect Charlie's got a good pedigree?"

"What's a pedigree?" said Arch.

"A family tree," I said.

"Any old tree does Charles," said Arch. "And don't call him Charlie."

He told me this years after the dog was dead. Arch told me he missed Charles something awful. Especially as he had all the money when he died and he passed on before he could go and dig it up and hand it over. But that's beside the point. The point is that Charles was waiting on the veranda of the pub that time at Muckadilla when Arch got into the argument with the three drovers who were taking this big mob of sheep down to Moree. New South Welshmen, they were, I mean, said Arch, nobody can help where they are born, but you don't have to go on living there after you know that there's a place like Queensland just a bit north. Not that I've got anything against New South Welshmen, but I wouldn't want one to marry my sister.

It turned out that these three blokes all had the smartest sheepdog in the world. They were standing arguing at the bar, and drinking raspberry in their rum, which should have warned Arch that they weren't Queenslanders, and the next thing he knew he was talking to them just as though they weren't foreigners. Really it started out with him quietly telling them that they were all mistaken. They wouldn't believe him, and one thing led to another, as things sometimes do in bars at places like Muckadilla. It finished up with Arch challenging the three of them to come out the back where the bull fed and try their luck. He was very debonair in his youth, says Arch, gay and reckless like that bloke D'Artagnan in *The Three Musketeers*, the only other bloke I know who challenged three blokes to fight him at the same time. Well, there was old Ban Ban Jackson at Biggenden that time, but nobody is ever going to tell that story.

So there was Arch ready to strip off his waistcoat and into these three blokes at the woodheap while the admiring dogs watched, when the parson came running out from the parlour and asked what the trouble was. When they explained it he said "Come, come," and things like that. He pointed out that fighting would only settle who was the best fighter, not whose dog was the smartest. He suggested that the dogs be given a trial, youngest first, and that if they cared to put a small wager on the result he would hold the stakes as an impartial observer. That's what he said. When Arch explained all this to Charles, Charles said that he was confident that he could beat two of the other dogs after listening to them talk, but that there was one big old red kelpie that he wasn't too sure about. Anyhow Arch made him give him the money, and they all put up a fiver a side and gave it to the parson to hold while they put the dogs through their paces.

At straight-out sheep work there wasn't anything between them. They could all cut a marked wether out of the mob and yard it by itself in no time. So it came down to fancy tricks. The youngest dog went up first. The drover pretended to be asleep on the ground beside his fire. The dog fetched some kindling, blew up the coals until the fire glowed, and filled the billy from the waterbag. Then it woke the drover when the billy boiled. A good standard average performance, but nothing to the competition that was there that day. The second drover laughed, and pretended to go to sleep. His dog did the same as the younger one, only it made the tea and poured a cup for the drover before it woke him. Fair enough. Then the third drover pretended to go to sleep. His dog, the old red kelpie, did all that the others had done, only it put a spoon of sugar in the tea, carried it over to the drover, blew on it till it was cool, and then woke him up. Arch could see it would be a close go but he needn't have worried. Charles did all the things that the other three dogs had done except that he milked a passing nanny goat as well and put milk in Arch's tea before he woke him, and then went back to the billy and poured out one for himself.

"Well, I don't know," said the parson. "I think we must eliminate the first two contestants. Let us proceed to a final test between the two remaining animals." The other two drovers wanted to argue but Arch had the other bloke on his side this time and they told the others to shut up. The parson went into the bar and got two old empty hock bottles that a passing loco driver had left there. These he placed side by side on the ground about three feet apart. Then he caught a blowfly out of the millions that were flying round the publican and marked it on the back with a spot of white paint and let it go again. Then he stood back and invited the dogs to put the fly into either of the two bottles.

The big red kelpie went first. He quartered back and forth with his belly close to the ground. He never barked. He shouldered the other blowflies aside, and when they got too thick he got up on their backs and ran across them in mid-air, and all the time he relentlessly drove that one marked blowfly towards the two bottles. Eventually he had it poised outside the neck of one of the bottles. He crouched motionless on the ground, menacing the blowfly. The blowfly stamped its forefoot at him, but it recognised its master and turned disconsolately and buzzed into the bottle, which the dog then corked and took to his master. Even Arch could scarce forebear to cheer.

Arch was worried. He knew that Charles was good, but it began to look as though he'd met his match at last in this big ugly red dog. The kelpie sneered at Charles and winked at the local dogs who had gathered to watch. A small lady fox terrier present was heard to remark that the kelpie was welcome to put his boots under her bed any time he felt like it. Arch looked at Charles in a worried sort of way. Charles just grinned back confidently at him and winked. The other drovers demanded a fresh blowfly as the one that was yarded was used to being worked by this and would be easier. The parson caught a real leggy big blowfly and barely touched it with the paint. The minute he let it go it went and sat on the big ugly red dog's back and sneered at Charles. Charles waited until the drover had emptied the other fly out of the bottle and put it back on the ground. Then he went into action.

First he flew into the big red kelpie and bit him until he screamed for mercy and headed back for camp, probably to make himself a mug of tea. This dislodged the blowfly. With deadly skill and cunning Charles worked the blowfly. He worked it in and out of the bystanders. Then he took it three times round the pub and then over to the railway station and back through the store. He ran it until its buzz fell off. Quickly he rounded up the buzz and chased it into one of the bottles, which he quickly corked. You couldn't see it but if you put the bottle to your ear you could hear it very faintly through the glass. Of course the blowfly couldn't fly very well without its buzz, so it was child's play to put it in the other bottle, which he also corked. Then he put the three drovers in an empty beer barrel that was standing nearby, and drove the bung in so they couldn't get out. Then he stopped and waited for Arch.

Arch said, "Well, it looks like Charles won. He's a real Queensland dog."

The parson looked a bit put out by this. "If it comes to that, I'm from across the border myself," he said.

Before Arch could offer to fight him, Charles had put him away too, but I'm not going to say where he drove the parson. Use your imagination. But before he locked him in he drove the stakes out of the parson's pocket and into Arch's. Then he shot round the front of the pub and came back leading the packhorse and the saddle-horse by the bridle, and Arch took the hint and rode out of there. So don't mention smart sheepdogs when you're round Arch. He had a better one once.

The Giant Mud Gudgeon

My Uncle Arch was in a patch of very dry country once. There were seven-year-old frogs there that had never learnt to swim. The place was full of trees that moved. You'd camp at night on a bare patch and you'd wake up next morning surrounded by shrubbery. Arch says they used to sort of shuffle along on their roots. They got that way following the dogs around. It was so dry out there that they only got forty points that time Noah had all the trouble with the flood.

When he went there first, said Arch, he was amazed to see that even the grasshoppers carried a cut lunch when they went out in the morning in case they didn't find any blades of grass. Everybody carried a waterbag wherever they went, even the clouds.

One real hot day Arch was sitting on the veranda of the pub, drinking his beer before it got cold. It was real hot even for that place. A dingo came down the main street chasing a rabbit and they were both walking. There were a lot of mirages trying to get into the shade of each other. Of course, it's a real hot town. When old Ten Gallon Jackson died and went to Hell, he sent back for his blankets and his overcoat. But that's beside the point.

The point is, Arch was sitting on the veranda in the shade, wringing out the flies that fell in his beer before he thew them away, when he saw this big black cloud coming over the horizon, pushing the mirages out of the way. It looked a funny sort of cloud, and it wasn't for a minute or two that he realised what was funny about it. Then he saw it wasn't carrying a waterbag.

"Hey, boys," he said. "There's a big black cloud coming and it's not carrying a waterbag!"

Pandemonium broke loose. Blokes left the pub and began walking slowly in all directions.

"What's all the fuss?" asked Arch, but nobody seemed to have time to answer. Arch could see the cloud still coming, getting bigger and higher and blacker, and now he could even hear it. It was making a rumbling noise like a coal train going over a viaduct. Then the blokes started coming back, mostly carrying stockwhips; but a few of them were carrying Barcoo Dogs.

Now, a Barcoo Dog isn't a dog, said Arch. It's a six inch circle of eight gauge fencing wire with seventeen tin lids on it that rattle like hell when you shake it. The blokes out on the Barcoo River invented it because you could work sheep round the yards with it, and you didn't have to feed it and it was there hanging on its nail when you wanted it instead of being busy courting like a real dog was liable to be busy doing. Also it didn't eat anything, which is a point to be considered out on the Barcoo River. Also, it was the only musical instrument they had if they couldn't yodel. But that's beside the point. The point is that these blokes were going to muster and draft stock, and there was no stock for miles.

Arch finished his beer and went to see what was going on. If there's a bit of fun around Arch likes to be in it. The cloud was grumbling like an angry bull in fly time by this; all the mirages were headed for the ranges and the ordinary clouds were sprinting off westward as fast as they could go, swags slung behind them.

Arch tripped a bloke that was running past and held him down until he explained what the trouble was. It seems that once every eight years this cloud comes down from Arnhem Land and rains on them from a very great height. They call this cloud the Gulfer out there, because it isn't so much a cloud as part of the Gulf of Carpentaria, and it brings all its contents with it. You've heard of those fishes that rain out of the sky in western

Queensland, haven't you? Well, these are normally only the fringe of the Gulfer. The real middle of it has dugongs, turtles, and all kinds of other wildlife. This bloke Arch was holding said that they had their stockwhips and Barcoo Dogs ready to round up the fish that were going to come down in the rain into the stockyards. Once they were in the holding pens they'd sort them out, some to be eaten straight away and the rest to be tethered in the billabong until they needed them. So Arch let the bloke go and went to get his own stockwhip to give them a hand. He hadn't had a feed of fish for six years.

The cloud covered the sky now from base to apex and on all sides. It grumbled and yelled like a hundred bullockies. It flashed lightning like two hundred grinding wheels. Then it split its seams and the rain started coming down like water out of fire hoses. Mixed up in the rain was a saltwater crocodile, a school of barramundi, a small dead coral reef complete with Crown of Thorns starfish, 1 234 561 banana prawns, a rowing boat, and two American oilmen. Also there were a lot of ordinary fishes like flatheads and grunters, but you get them everywhere.

The blokes from the pub started yelling and cracking their whips and rattling their Barcoo Dogs and yodelling as they rounded up the fish into the holding paddock, then into the wings of the yard. They got the lot in and slammed the sliprails closed. It was a good catch. The cloud seemed to have lost all its spark and most of its grumble by this, except for one corner that was carrying on in a most odd way, like a Cock-eyed Bob with a knot in it. The other blokes all downed their whips and their Dogs and headed back for the pub, but Arch stayed leaning over the rails admiring the fish.

The cloud started to pull up its anchors and push off, but as it went the twisty bit suddenly pulled its plug out and rained harder than any of the other bits of cloud had, and riding down on the splash came this giant mud gudgeon. It was only about eight foot long, said Arch, but it had a girth like a Brahman-Hereford cross bullock, and its eyes were lit up like brazing torches.

As soon as it hit the ground it swam straight to the stockyards and started to drop the sliprails. When the crocodile got in its way it belted it sideways with a careless flick of one of its fins. The crocodile cannoned off the police station and ricocheted into the little house behind the pub where it frightened seven bells out of Dry Blower Lawson who was asleep in there at the time. Dry Blower set out rapidly for the sunset, followed by the crocodile which soon caught up and passed him because he was wearing his pants round his ankles like a pair of hobbles. He'd probably still be going except that his braces caught in a tree-stump and that eventually brought him to a halt.

Meanwhile the giant mud gudgeon had got into the stockyard and was gobbling up every fish in sight, except for the banana prawns which were very toey and jumped around like those blokes in Melbourne who play what they call football because they haven't heard about League. Arch quickly made a noose in the end of his stockwhip and quietly snuck up behind the mud gudgeon. He cracked his own variation of the Queensland Flash and lassoed the fish with the cracker. Then he took a quick turn round a handy corner post with the slack, and it's just as well he did.

A soon as the stockwhip brought it up short the big fish really began to put on its turn. It bucked and pranced like a billy goat. It stood on its tail and tried to throw the bait. It got a bit of slack on the line and tried to break it. Arch says it's just as well he plaited that whip himself, or it might have given way under the tremendous strain. What did give way was the fencepost, an enormous big lump of ironbark, and the mud gudgeon scuttled off across country dragging behind it the corner post, Arch, sixteen panels of fencing, and the pub veranda that they picked up as they went past.

Now you know how the Diamantina River got dug. The mud gudgeon still lives there but you don't need to be frightened of it any more. Just wave your stockwhip at it and it goes for its life.

Cyril and the Termites

My Uncle Arch was heading up from Broken Hill to Burketown once to get a job with old Skeleton Harris bringing a mob of beasts down to the Channels for fattening. He was just poking along up between Cheepie and Boulia when he ran into this anthill country. You know those magnetic white ants they have over in the Territory, that build their nests running north and south, or south and north, depending on which way you're going, said Arch. Well, these were pretty much the same sort of ants, only much bigger and tougher. They used to build their nests facing east and west, which wasn't much value to anybody riding north or south. I mean, with the Territory nests you could sort of slide your way past them, but with these ones you had to keep jumping over them, which was difficult even for the horse Arch had at the time, and it was a good one. Besides which the ants used to sit on top of their nests and snap at the horse's legs as it went over, and this worried Arch. It worried the horse, too, and after a couple of days in that country the horse used to be getting round tucking up its skirts like a sheila wading a creek. Every night when he camped, says Arch, he had to paint a ring of creosote round the horse's legs and his own and they both had to sleep standing up, to make sure they would still be there in the morning. It was terribly frustrating country for Charles, Arch's dog, too. Miles between trees. And they weren't very big trees, either, and they mostly only came out at night.

On the evening of the third day Arch was getting near the northern boundary of the ants' territory when he came upon this teamster. The teamster had six horses, four rings of iron about five feet across, a dog, and a billy can, a frying pan, an enamel mug, and two thousand three hundred and fifty-one bottles of rum, and a half. Arch said good day to him and he said good day to Arch, and asked him if he'd like a drink of rum. Arch said he didn't mind, and one thing led to another and he decided he'd camp there for the night with Cyril, that was this bloke's name. Now, it's not very often that you come across a bloke in the bush with such a funny-looking outfit, and Arch decided privately that this Cyril must be having some difficulties in his life, things looking as they did. So he said to Cyril that night, "You seem to be having a bit of trouble, mate. Seeing you've been so hospitable to me, maybe I could help. What's up?"

Cyril started to cry and said that he had this team and wagon he'd been saving up to buy since he was thirteen, and it was all paid for, and the first loading he'd picked up was for the pub at Wayback, and he'd been going along well and making good time till he camped at this place one night. There had been a lot of kegs of beer in the load, as well, he said. It wasn't so bad when he camped for the night; he'd seen the ants' nests but he hadn't taken much notice of them, just ate his salt beef and damper and went to sleep as usual. In the night a few white ants had come along and started chewing at the wagon, but they weren't doing much good, until one ugly little white ant started to chew on one of the beer barrels. Of course it got full on the wood, and went and told all the other white ants, who hadn't had a beer for years, and it's pretty hot out there. Of course they sent messages to all their relations, and the whole mob of them came, and if you think the picnic races at Brunette Downs is a spree you never saw anything like about five million drunken white ants dancing and chewing and fighting and all in dead silence, so Cyril never woke up until the next morning. By that time they had cleaned up the beer, kegs and all, the cases and straw packing from round the rum, and the whole of the wagon except for the iron tyres, and even these were looking a bit frayed. He said it was just as well there was a lead cap over the corks of the rum bottles or they would have got that too, but a few of them had a bit of a nibble and died of lead poisoning right off, and the word went round to leave them alone. So there he was, and had been for a fortnight. He said he'd had two hundred dozen bottles to start with but that they were diminishing a bit while he sat round trying to think of a way out of his predicament. After saying all this Cyril stopped crying and reached out for the bottle again in an absent-minded way.

Arch asked him if he had had any more trouble from the ants since and Cyril said that the ants all had such terrible hangovers the next day when they had slept off their excesses that the word seemed to have got round that it was poison he was carrying, and that some of them had even moved their nests a bit further away. Arch mentioned that nearly the same thing had happened to him once, only the other way round, when he had lost his team of bullocks and been left with only the wagon and the load, and thirty mile to go to get it to Gympie.

He'd used a bread poultice to draw it and Cyril said couldn't he do the same thing here and Arch was forced to admit that while the same trick would work it wouldn't be possible because he didn't have enough flour with him. However, he said that he would think it over, and that sooner or later he was bound to come up with something, so they finished the bottle they were working on and went to sleep lying down, which was a relief after the last two nights for Arch and his horse, and for Charles too.

Arch admitted to me when he told me the story that he knew straight away what they ought to do, but that he thought that he should appear to give the matter deep consideration; and anyway a man would be an idiot just to get up and ride away from a situation like that. After about a week, though, Cyril was getting so depressed that Arch could see it was now or never, and anyway, he wasn't as thirsty as he had been. So he went across to the four biggest white ants' nests near the camp, and started talking to Cyril in a loud voice about what a lovely old wooden building the pub at Wayback was, and how he was going to go straight there and try to get some help, and how lucky it was that these ants hadn't found out about it, or they would have gone over there and cleaned it up by now. Of course the white ants heard him, and they all stopped chewing on the tough old gidgee that was all they had to eat, and their mandibles started dribbling at the thought of all that beautiful milled timber, just the difference between a fillet steak and a bit of shin beef to a white ant. So when Arch loaded up he was delighted to see a team of white ants watching him furtively from behind gibbers, and over the top of the potholes in the track. He pretended not to notice, just got on his horse and rode away, winking at Cyril and riding slow so the ants could keep up with him. Three days later, just before they came in sight of the Wayback pub, Arch knocked a couple of mickey bulls over and quickly skinned them. He then cut the greenhide into thin strips until he had hundreds of little thin strips of greenhide. You should have heard those ants moan when the pub came in sight and they saw it was only made of old galvanised iron on a channel iron frame. But before they could turn for home in disgust Arch yelled "Righto Charles", and Charles rounded the mob of them up. Arch lassoed them by the hundreds, and tied them to the pub before they could make their escape. Then he got out his new stockwhip and cracked the Queensland Flash.

Those ants were big and tough, and they were hungry and disappointed and they were keen to get home. Besides, they had Charles snapping at their heels and Arch cracking the Queensland Flash all round them.

They dug in their toes so the claypans were ground into bulldust, and they started for home pulling the pub behind them. They were so disgruntled, said Arch, that they reached Cyril before daylight the next morning, travelling by the light of the moon, which shines brighter out there than it does on the coast. And there were no trees to get in the road either, because the ants ate them as they came across them, and the gibbers formed rollers, just as he had planned, and they travelled so smooth that the publican and his wife and two daughters never even woke up.

As soon as he got within cooee of Cyril's camp, Arch whipped out his knife and cut the traces. The pub settled gently down, and Arch and Cyril carried the remaining rum quietly into the bar. Then they woke the publican and demanded a drink. The country out there is so big and similar to itself that the publican never even noticed the move, and the insurance paid for the beer. But, said Arch, he has never been game to go back to that country in case he dies there. He says it makes his blood run cold when he thinks what those ants would do to his coffin if ever he was planted near them, and as for his carcass, it just doesn't bear thinking on.

Scotty, Maria, Onions, and the Dutchman

When my Uncle Arch was cutting cane in North Queensland at a place called Eubenangee, he was the gun cutter in the area and he was much respected in the district for his truthfulness and industry. Cane was harder to cut in those days, Arch says, because of the wild boars and crocodiles and taipans that kept springing out at you. The soil was so fertile that the cane was still growing while you were cutting it. The pumpkins used to keep them awake at night because the soil was so good that the vines grew very fast, and it was nothing to have a vine climb up the wall of the cane barracks and drag the pumpkins across the galvanised iron roof, which disturbed their rest a fair bit. That soil was so rich that blokes who cut in bare feet often finished the season three inches taller than when they started, just from standing in the mud.

Uncle Arch was cutting with a mate called Moses O'Flaherty, a half-Chinese bloke, but everybody called him Scotty because he couldn't stand whisky. He was a fine big strapping fellow, said Arch, and he was a good cutter, and you couldn't meet a nicer bloke. They were working a two-man area; actually it was a three-man cut, but Arch was a gun as I said, and Scotty wasn't bad, so they had no trouble keeping ahead of the job.

One of the farms on the run they were cutting belonged to a Spaniard called Diego de something or other, though everybody called him Onions and he didn't know why, though his daughter Maria tried to tell him often enough. His wife was dead and Maria was housekeeping for him. Arch says she was a good-looking sheila with big brown eyes like a poddy calf and a lot of shiny long black hair. She must have been a good sort because Arch tells me that him and Scotty used to have a bath every night and put on clean flannel shirts and dungarees and go up to the house to play euchre with Onions and his daughter. Looking at him now you'd never believe it but Arch says he was a striking figure of a man himself in those days, and he used to grease his hair with a bit of mutton fat he kept for rubbing on the stitching of his boots to keep them from rotting in the wet season, and pretty himself up in other ways.

Now, though Arch and Scotty were such good mates they were a bit crooked on each other over this Maria, and it began to show. It was the dead opposite of those stories you read about in books where two blokes get shook on the same sheila, how they both sneak off and nobly join the Foreign Legion, and one gets killed and dies with the other bloke holding him up, and the other bloke goes home and marries the sheila and everything's jake because it's the one she didn't love that snuffed it anyway. The only place Arch and Scotty ever snuck off to was the Garradunga pub, and they always snuck off together like mates should, and Scotty never passed out with Arch holding him up because Arch usually passed out about the same time. They never did go the knuckle on each other over this sheila either, but they did start to get a bit crooked on each other because Scotty was a fine-looking fellow, and good-looking too, and Arch was a bit jealous, because while no one can deny that he is a striking-looking bloke he's not what you might call handsome. On the other hand, as he was the gun cutter in the area, old Onions was a bit his way, because he reckoned that if his daughter had to get married it better be to a good toiler. So this gave Arch a bit of a leg-in.

Well, Scotty got a bit maggoty about this and started to crack the pace on a bit in the paddock, until it was all Arch could do to stay ahead of him. After a fortnight of building up pace they found that they were cutting eleven tons a day each in a paddock of standover third ratoon Badila, so they decided that they had better settle who was the faster, and also the business of Maria, once and for all.

The way they did it was as follows. Old Onions had a little three acre paddock of sugar cane, his pride and joy. This paddock was the best soil on the place, so rich you could spread it on bread and eat it instead of butter. Well, the two of them went to Onions one night and everything was arranged so that they were to start cutting it the next morning. Onions was to mark the paddock off into two halves, they were to start cutting at daylight, and the bloke who finished first was to have open slather with Maria. This suited everybody, but by an oversight they forgot to tell Maria about it.

Well, the following morning they lined up at the barrier. You know what it's like early in the morning in October in North Queensland. A sort of green light in the sky, and the stars going out one by one, and everything dripping wet with dew. The little honeyeaters tune up, the old swamp pheasants are drumming in the swamps, and it's the one hour in the twenty-four when you feel a bit cool. Onions was to be referee and start them, and make sure they cut low and topped high. So they went into it.

They were both young and hard as nails and in good nick. The cane was clean and they had got a good burn. As soon as daylight showed properly they were away and Arch says he found himself cutting as he'd never cut before. But it was no good. Scotty was in training and stayed with him. When dark came and the last stools fell they were still running dead level, and it was a dead heat.

It didn't matter much though, Arch says, because Maria picked that day to run away with a Dutchman who was so ignorant that he had never even heard of the little fellow countryman of his who sat with his hand in the dyke all night. Scotty and Arch were so disgusted about it that they went off streaming tin on the Tableland. Arch says he bumped into Maria about five years ago and he's glad because she weighs about eighteen stone now and has a voice like a saw going through a knot in a pine board, not to mention the way she laughs. He only wishes Scotty was alive to celebrate their escape, that the horse hadn't dragged him that time at Biloela. The Dutchman died years ago too.

The French Chef

My Uncle Arch was down at Southport once in the days before bathing suits lost their skirts and Stradbroke Island got washed in halves. He was blueing the last of a shearing cheque when he met this big gun banana bender. At that time all the bananas in Queensland grew straight out from the bunch; not like the imported Fijian bananas that were bent and fetched higher prices because they were imported and therefore better than any home grown ones. There was a mob of shrewdies living up Nerang way who woke up to this. They started off by changing the name of their district to Fiji, then bending their bananas and sending them off to Sydney in cases marked "GROWN IN FIJI". They used to bend their bananas by holding them in a jet of steam until they were soft and then bending them one by one. There was a lot of blokes bending them on contract, and this bloke Arch was sinking schooners with was a gun bender. He said Arch could make his fare back to Mount Perry in a week easily and he'd get him a start. As it was daylight by then they didn't bother to sleep it off. They just topped up with two raw eggs in Worcester sauce and they were off.

Well, Arch got a start without any trouble and he toiled away all day and made a few bob, but that night he felt sore and thought there must be an easier way of doing it. He often says now that he doesn't know what got into him, but he had a good idea, so instead of getting stuck into it with the other benders the next morning, he clouted onto a bunch of bananas and out of sight round the back of the bending shed. He hung the bananas on a kind of gallows over half a kerosene tin of boiling water for five minutes; then bent the whole bunch at once by running his hands down the outside from top to bottom. This was mechanisation, and he bent enough bananas that day to pay his fare back to Mount Perry and his humpy in the Goodnight Scrub. Just as well he did.

Now, this cocky was a shrewdie and he took a wake-up to Arch early on and sneaked round and watched what Arch was doing from behind the guava bushes near the dunny. When he saw how Arch came to be bending such big tallies he fired all his benders and did all his own bending from then on. Not only that, he told all the other cockies in the area about it, so all the benders were out of work. This made all the benders very crooked on Arch, the man who introduced automation to banana bending. Arch reckoned he rolled his bluey in a hurry and lit out for Mount Isa, and it's just as well he did, or there's no telling what the Union might have done to him. There was some talk of hanging him over a kero tin of boiling water and leaving him permanently bent.

So Arch reckons he had as good a reason as anybody for going to Mount Isa. When he got there he reckoned he'd found a mouth to hell that those old Greeks didn't know about; what with the stink of burning sulphides from the roasting plant, the heat and dust, and the look of the blokes getting round the place. At any rate, he saw the head serang for a start, and was told that the only job going was cooking for the contract men. There was one snag; a little skinny bloke with melancholy eyes and a weeping moustache had showed up looking for a job too. He was a Frog from Paris called Pierre, who had been running two different sheilas in different suburbs that found out about each other at the same time. Instead of fighting over him they went out together looking for him. His mate had spotted them and drummed him in time for him to blow through, so he had as good a reason for going to Mount Isa as anybody. "Mong Jew, women!" he used to say.

This Pierre was a scranbasher from way back, he reckoned, but the head serang was a sport so he made it up that the two of them should each cook a feed and the contract men could bog into it, and then vote for whoever they wanted to be their cook. He didn't care so long as the men were happy. So Arch and Pierre headed for the cookhouse for the great competition.

Now it turned out later that this Froggy bloke Pierre had been a sort of gun chef where he came from, and he burst into tears when he saw the cookhouse. Arch had to comfort him. He felt sorry for the poor fellow, who was used to a few conveniences. It was Arch who split up the gidgee and ghost gum logs and got the range started. To give him his due, the little bloke was no piker. He even put on a white apron, the first one that had ever been seen in Mount Isa, and buckled in to making little flaky pastries and emu egg omelets and other interesting things. Arch could see that it was going to be a close go as he boiled the corn beef and put the carrots in to soozle in the juice. The Frenchman turned out four sponge cakes that nearly floated off the window sill, while Arch boiled up a whopper of a brownie in his spare shirt. Pierre did his best with some brown mud out of a tin labelled COFFEE and Arch stewed up some tea in a kerosene tin and sweetened it up with a dollop of molasses. Then they went out and hammered on the old crowbar, and the mob came roaring over from the barracks and bogged in.

Arch reckoned he'd done the job in, because the Frenchman could obviously cook rings round him. He said so, and Pierre said calmly, "Wee wee", which is Frog for "too right". But they'd forgotten one thing. The blokes they were feeding had lived most of their lives on Barcoo sandwiches and Condamine rolls and tucker like that. So they were a bit careful of the strange tucker, but Arch had done a fair job on familiar stuff, damper

and corned beef and carrots and brownie and tea. So they all voted for Arch. The little bloke said, "Mong jew!" and was going to fade out but in the meantime Arch had met an old mate of his called Knuckles O'Hara who was going out fencing to Victoria River Downs and offered Arch partnership. So Arch went. Before he went he taught the little bloke to cook corn beef and carrots and make a brownie in his spare shirt, also how to make a Barcoo Sandwich, which is a curlew between two sheets of bark, and a Condamine roll, which is a goanna rolled up in a damper, and other bush tucker. Pierre caught on fast so the contract men didn't mind.

So Arch went out into the Territory again, and stayed there until he had another cheque to blue. They don't have to bend Queensland bananas by hand any more. An old bloke up on Buderim Mountain had the arthuritis so bad his bananas caught it off him, and all the other fruit-cockies got suckers from him to save having to bend by hand. You hardly ever see it being done now. And Arch said he's learnt his lesson about having bright ideas, so that's why he hasn't told anybody about the way he's worked out that a bloke can shear two sheep at once and sweep up the board at the same time. He says that it might lead to bad feeling in Union circles, and he is a staunch Unionist.

Uncle Arch and the Bower Bird

My Uncle Arch was out near the town of Emerald once. He was looking for sapphires. He spent all his time digging holes in the ground where the sapphires might be, but mostly they were somewhere else. He didn't find many because of this. It was very dry. There was one waterhole left on the creek where there was a little bit of water, but it wasn't going to last long because the bushes used to sneak down for a drink when nobody was watching them.

Arch was digging in his mine one morning when he heard a noise. He looked over the top of the hole like a goanna looking over a log, but he couldn't see anything. He looked up into the wattle trees and the bloodwood trees and the brigalow trees. Nothing. Then he saw a little head watching him around the trunk of a gum tree. It was a dark blue feathery head. It belonged to a bower bird that lived near him.

"Got any blue stones?" asked the bower bird.

Arch got very cranky with the bower bird. He knew they liked blue things to decorate their bowers with. He knew that, if there were any blue sapphires around, the bird would pinch them to decorate its bower. But he wanted the sapphires for himself, so he said, "Get away, bird. You've got a head like a castor-oil bottle!"

This made the bower bird very angry. Nobody likes castor oil, so the bird knew he was throwing off at it. It took a very quick running dive for the dirt Arch had thrown out of the hole, snapped up a great big blue sapphire in its little pointy beak, and went for its life before Arch could get out of the hole. He swore at it of course, but the bird didn't care. It had the blue sapphire to decorate its bower with.

This started the war between my Uncle Arch and the bower bird. Each of them was too clever for the other one, so after a couple of weeks both were very tired. But neither had managed to catch the other. This bird used to hide in the bush near where Arch was working and laugh just loud enough for him to hear it. When Arch went charging off to try to hit it with a stick, the bird would run to his mine and pinch the sapphires.

Arch, on the other hand, used to spend all his spare time trying to find the bird's bower so he could pinch all the blue sapphires the bird had found. The bird got a bit exhausted, moving its bower around all the time in case Arch found it. Both of them were pretty cranky with the other by this time, and they weren't enjoying themselves very much. The bower bird had a crick in its neck from looking back over its shoulder to make sure Arch wasn't sneaking up on it from behind. Arch had sore feet from tramping everywhere through the bush looking for the bower.

One day when Arch was creeping through a very thick patch of bushes, he saw something blue on the ground. He got his waddy ready and crept along until he could reach it. He hit it hard with his club. He was surprised when it turned out that what he had hit was a blue beanie on the head of another sapphire miner who was down his hole in the ground, peacefully digging. The other sapphire miner got very cranky with Arch, too, and chased him up and down Tomahawk Creek all afternoon, trying to hit him on the head with a tree he had picked up. The bower bird didn't help. It flew along near Arch, laughing at him and telling him to run harder and telling the other miner where Arch was hiding. It was dark before Uncle Arch got safely home to his tent. He was very tired from running and very angry with the bower bird because he blamed his troubles on it.

One day when Uncle Arch was in the town of Emerald, he saw a blue glass necklace in Woolworths, going cheap. He got an idea about how he might use it to catch the bower bird. He bought the necklace and hurried back to his camp. Getting the tin of treacle he used to spread on his damper, he balanced it on the branch of a tree. Then he tied a thin, strong piece of fishing line onto the tin. The other end he tied to the blue glass necklace and put it on the ground underneath the tree. Then he hid and watched.

Soon the bower bird came sneaking through the bushes to have a look at his camp. It got terribly excited when it saw the blue beads shining in the sunlight. It dived out of the bushes and ran across the camp clearing as fast as it could go. It snatched up the necklace and started to run away with it. You can just imagine how surprised it was when the fishing line came tight and pulled the tin of treacle off the branch! The treacle poured from the tin all over the bower bird. It stuck its feet to the ground and its wings got stuck to its sides so it couldn't fly. Dead leaves stuck all over it. Little bits of sand and dirt clung to its bright blue feathers. Millions of flies came and walked all over it because it was so sweet and a lot of them got stuck to the bird, too. When Arch came out of the bushes where he had been hiding, the flies got alarmed and tried to fly away. It was no good. The bird was too heavy for them to lift, though they nearly got it off the ground a couple of times.

Arch sat down on a log and laughed and laughed at the sandy, leafy, dirty, grassy, treacly, fly-ey, sticky bower bird. The bird just sat there stickily and looked back at him. It couldn't get away. It thought its time had come.

Just then Uncle Arch had a visitor. It was his old Aboriginal friend, Black Peter.

"What are you doing?" asked Peter.

"This cheeky bower bird has been pinching my blue sapphires, so I've caught him, and now I'm going to cure him of having sticky fingers," said Arch.

Peter looked closely at the bower bird.

"He's got sticky fingers, all right," he said. "Everything else, too!"

"Treacle," said Arch.

"Poor little feller," said Peter. "Hey, I got an idea. Why

should you two go on fighting all the time? He only wants the blue ones. What about the red and green and yellow sapphires? They're just as good as the blue ones. Why don't you give him all the blue ones you find, and he can bring you all the others he finds? He doesn't want them. You could swap them. That way there'd be no more fighting!"

Arch thought about this for a while. So did the bower bird. They looked at each other and then, after a bit, they both started to laugh like mad.

"You do look funny!" said Arch.

"So do you," said the bird.

"Is it a deal, then? I'll give you all the blue stones if you'll bring me the others?" asked Arch.

"It's a deal," agreed the bower bird. But they couldn't shake hands because the bird was too sticky.

Peter took the bird down to the waterhole, frightening some bushes that had crept in for a quiet drink. He washed the flies, sand, dirt, treacle, leaves and grass off and its coat of feathers was shining blue once more. It flew away among the trees while he went back to have a billy of tea with Arch.

After that, Arch did very well for a while. Because its beak was so close to the ground, the bird found a lot more stones than Arch, and it brought most of them to him. He gave it the glass beads for nothing, and the bird was very pleased with them. They got to be good mates after that and often had a good laugh about the troubles they had had when they first knew each other.

Arch tried to give Peter some sapphires because it had been his idea that they stop fighting and help each other. But that wise old black man just smiled said, "What's the use of those stones? A man can't eat them, he can't drink them, and they won't keep you warm at night. No thanks, I'll leave them to you cranky white blokes."

"And to the bower birds?" asked Arch, grinning.

"Ah, those little fellers like them to play with. That's all they're good for, really," said Peter.

Perhaps he was right.

The Two Sisters

Just about the time World War II started, my Uncle Arch stopped working his goldmine at the Dead Goat and started dyeing his hair and shaved off his beard and only left his moustache, and he dyed that too and then tried to get into the Army again, but they wouldn't have him, he was too old. So he went to live at my Uncle Geordie's house at Elliott Heads because my Uncle Geordie was a wharfie and joined the Army and went away.

Arch used to go fishing up the river in his old flattie then go up to Bundaberg in his old Mystery Overland he had cut down into a ute to raffle any decent fish he caught around the pubs.

When he had a bit of money for petrol he used to sneak off to Gin Gin and Maryborough and places like that where they didn't know him and try to join the Army again, but they wouldn't have him either. He got real cranky about it and one day he asked the bloke how they expected to win the bloody war without decent bullock-drivers but the bloke just laughed. So he gave up trying to join the Army for a while and just stuck to fishing and going crook.

He had about a dozen chooks in a bit of a yard at the back of Uncle Geordie's house with a big game rooster that used to chase away the hawks and goannas that came to steal the eggs. The chooks used to walk about the paddock among the big basalt boulders and spent the day scratching and eating little lizards and those big brown grasshoppers that live at Elliott Heads which was very good for the chooks and gave them a lot of exercise. Arch always reckoned that after you ate eggs like those hens used to lay it spoiled ordinary eggs for you. They had a lot of body to them and were full of protein and lizard and vitamins and grasshoppers and that.

He had names for all the hens but his favourite was a scraggy old red one named Maggie who had a baldy sort of patch on the front of her neck who was the best sitter of them all when she went clucky. She always used to lay her eggs in the sawdust box in the dunny down the back of the house and when she was clucky she'd fly at anything that came near her nest. Arch reckoned that if she'd had teeth she'd have been as good a watchdog as Charles had been, rest his soul.

One morning after he'd been there a few months a couple of his mates came to visit him for a bit of a yarn and a few rums. One of them was his old fishing mate John the Yabby, who only had one hand but had a big steel hook where the other one used to be, and the other one was the son of the same old bloke Percy Stanley that Arch and the other young blokes used to pinch the watermelons from that I told you about before. Young Perc was just like his old man, sort of little and skinny and droopy-looking, but don't let that fool you. Because after his father had got married he'd run away from home and he'd been working on the cattle stations ever since out round Tenningering and Boolbunda and Bymingo and those places and he'd got to be the best horse-breaker around the place. He could sit anything from a four-year-old mickey bull to the worst bucker and never get tossed. You know about John the Yabby, I told you about how him and Arch and Mullet-Gut Olaf went fishing once. But that's beside the point.

The point is that these blokes drove up in Perc's old Model A Ford and took the three bottles of rum out and went looking for Arch and found him sneaking round and round the fowlhouse with a dirty big waddy. When they asked him what he was doing he said he'd seen a big brown snake poking round the nests after the eggs and that he was looking for it. But when he saw the bottles they'd brought he threw the stick away quick and they came upstairs and he got an old peanut butter glass and two glass cups like we used to get during the war and they started to knock over the first bottle and talk about the mistakes the generals and those blokes running the war were making at the time.

The others used to defer to Arch a bit about this because he'd been to France in 1917 and so was an expert at all this. Then after they'd got stuck into the second bottle a bit they thought they'd go up to Bundaberg and try to join the Army again but the sergeant there wouldn't have them even though John showed him how he could hook blokes with his steel hook and tore the sergeant's shirt right off his back.

They finished the second bottle on the way back to Elliott Heads, and stopped noticing the sandflies and had a feed of fish, then they had a cup of tea and finished the third bottle. They decided to have an early night so they could get up early and fish the early morning rising tide along near the Old Man Rock so the other two unrolled their swags and Arch crept into the old stretcher bed he'd found in a cocky's cane-barracks when no one was watching. But before they settled in to sleep Perc said he had to go down back and visit the little house before turning in.

Arch offered him the hurricane lamp but he said he knew the way, so off he went. But in a couple of minutes they heard him yell out so they grabbed the lamp to go and see what was the matter. Maybe he'd fallen down the well. Or something. But he met them holding up his moleskins with one hand and told them he'd been bitten on the stern when he was reversing up to the seat and he hoped it wasn't the snake Arch had been chasing. This shook the others almost sober so they laid him out face down on the table and got the lamp for a look and sure enough they saw two little puncture marks on his bottom.

Well, they were a bit mystified what to do because you can't put a tourniquet around a bloke's bum; but they knew the rest of the drill for a snake-bite so they got Arch's old blade razor and operated on him, and made a fair sort of slash, though it was a bit bigger than they meant to make because, as Arch said, it was Perc's fault because he wouldn't keep still. Then they sucked and spat and packed the hole with Condy's crystals and tore up Arch's singlet and strapped him up the best they could. Then Arch and John decided they'd better get the snake, so they left Perc swearing at them, and Arch got the rusty old Dutch hoe Geordie used for cultivating his tomatoes when he wasn't in the Army and John took the lamp and they set off on their mission of ruthless revenge.

It turned out to be all a bit awkward when they got to the dunny because they found it wasn't a snake at all but old Maggie the clucky hen that was sitting in the sawdust box and she was still wild at blokes that came near a respectable hen when she was in the process of preparing to raise a family. She was going to have a go at them too, but they left her to it. When they broke the news to Perc, though, it was amazing how cranky he got; especially after a day or so when he ate standing up but his bum wasn't getting any better so they had to take him to the hospital lying on his belly on a mattress in the back of Arch's old Mystery Overland. Then he got upset even more when the doctor laughed when he was disinfecting him and sewing him up, and he didn't talk to either Arch or John for years afterwards.

Well, there were two sisters in the ward where Perc finished up and they both took a bit of a shine to him. Neither of them were what you might call raving beauties, they were both about Perc's age and they were pretty good mates with each other, and he took a shine to both of them too, and he told them what a good horseman he was and how nothing alive could throw him and they were impressed; but unfortunately Perc wasn't allowed to get out of bed so when he needed to go they brought him a bedpan. Now, Perc had never seen one of these things before but he got into the saddle and next thing you know he went head-over-tip sideways, thrown for the first time in his life. The old bloke in the bed opposite laughed so much he fell out of bed and broke his leg but he said it was worth it.

But neither of the sisters laughed at him, they just straightened him out and showed him a lot of affection in a most friendly manner, and you could see that Perc was thinking about this, said Arch. These ladies weren't a bit jealous of each other and were prepared to share Perc between them; and of course Perc had never had much to do with women before and didn't know how they can't be trusted, said Arch. The upshot of it all was that the three of them all went to live together after Perc recovered. There wasn't any foolish talk about complications like getting married and they lived happily ever afterwards.

Arch got a job in the Civil Construction Corps shortly afterwards and he tells me that he practically built that road from Charters Towers down to Blair Athol single-handed because of this. I don't know what happened to Maggie the Hen, Geordie told me she was gone when he came back to being a wharfie after the war was over. John the Yabbie went back on the wharves with him and was very useful loading wool because he didn't need a bale hook.

Great Uncle Angus

My Uncle Arch was digging for opal once between Toompine and Thargomindah, and it was hard sinking. That's mostly a red sandstone, mud rock, and claypan country down there south of Cheepie. The opal was about forty feet down, and he was sinking the shaft by hand, with picks and bars, because if you put a charge of fracteur in you shatter any opal in a quarter of a mile radius, like the blokes did the chrysoprase up north of Rockhampton, Arch says.

He wasn't boss on this particular job. He was sort of between contracts at the time, so he'd gone out to help my Great Uncle Angus, who owned the claim. Angus was a thin whiskery bloke who used to work as topman for Arch. He sharpened and re-hardened the pick heads, wound the buckets up and down on the windlass, and drove down to Eulo in the sulky when they needed tucker. They used to get five gallons of rum from the grocer every month so as not to catch the Cuttaburra Cramps, a disease much dreaded by the local inhabitants, and the symptoms of which are much too dreadful to relate here.

Anyway, the two of them were sitting beside the fire late one afternoon when this big sort of aeroplane came belting down out of the sky and screamed to a halt about a hundred yards away, blowing the tea billy full of dust and nearly blowing the fire out. Angus wasn't very struck on machinery. He'd seen the train a couple of times at Cunnamulla, and once he'd got real game and had a ride on the mail truck, but he used to say that if God intended us to ride in machinery He'd have given us wheels. At any rate, that was the limit of his mechanical knowledge. Arch wasn't much better then, though he is now. After all, who was it mended Donald Campbell's big blue car at Lake Eyre that time, using a safety pin, an old garter he kept for sentimental reasons, and the click part of a ballpoint pen? But that's beside the point.

The point is that this big shiny thing came out of the sky and blew dust into their tucker, as I said. Angus looked at it, then he shook his pipe out and said "What is it, Arch?"

Arch thought about it for a while and then he said, "Busted if I know."

The thing was about the shape of the lid of a camp oven or a tin pie-dish, round and flattish with a sort of bump in the middle. It was made out of shiny metal and had portholes round the side. It was about sixty yards across and it hummed. I don't mean it smelt, I mean it made a humming sort of noise.

"It might be one of them hoptycopters I was reading about," said Arch.

"We better have a nip, anyhow," said Angus. "This bloody tea's like mud, now."

So he emptied the quartpots into the dog's drinking dish to settle, and poured them both a nip. The big aeroplane made a sort of buzzing noise and part of the side unfolded like steps, and a bloke and a girl wearing skindiving suits came down the stairs and wandered across to the camp, picking their way through the bindi-eyes and spinifex. The old blue dog was sneaking round behind them to heel them like he did the income tax man that time, but Angus pitched a bit of firewood at him, and told him to go and lie down. There was time enough for that later when they found out what this bloke wanted.

"Good day," said Arch. "We can't offer you a drink of tea, you blew it full of dust. Would you like a nip of rum, though?"

Angus didn't say anything, he wasn't much of a one for talking any time, and he was shy, not being up on social discourse, because he'd been born under a camel wagon near Tennant Creek and lived most of his life in the Simpson Desert, which may have accounted for his thirst. Arch reckons he only needed a drink of water once a week, but rum was a different matter.

"How quaint," said the sheila. "How simple these people are."

Arch was a bit bewildered at this, but he finished his drink and poured a fresh one for the girl into his quartpot, and handed it to her, and got a clean milk tin and gave the bloke his in it because Angus never lent his quartpot to anybody except the dog.

The bloke sniffed the rum, then he sipped it, and turned a bit pale. "It's undoubtedly some form of ritual observance," he told the girl. "It's to test the strength and resolution of the guest at the hearth." He turned back to Arch and Angus and said, "I pledge you!" Then he swallowed the rum, turned green, and sat down heavily on the horsecollar and wheezed for a bit.

The girl sipped her drink more carefully.

"Flying Doctor, are you?" asked Arch. "While you're

here there's this sort of indigestion I get about eight o'clock every night. Rum don't seem to help it, either, in fact, the more I drink the worse it gets. Just here, it gets me." He pointed to his belt buckle, which was real silver and in the shape of a horseshoe.

The bloke had his breath back by now. "No, I am not the Flying Doctor," he said. "My name is Leri, and the girl is Mora. We come from the star Betelguese in our flying saucer."

"What's a saucer?" said Angus. "Hey, you wouldn't be any relation to old Dogger O'Leary at Betoota, are you? I lent him a saddlegirth in nineteen-ten and he hasn't brought it back. I suppose it'd be wore out by now, anyhow."

"We are no relation," said Leri.

"Do that again," said Arch.

"What?" said Leri.

"There you go," said Arch. "You talk without opening your mouth. Did you see him, Uncle Angus?"

"Yeah," said Angus. "Saw a bloke do it once before, in a travelling show at Wilcannia. Come up the Darling on a paddle steamer. Had a doll called Bertie, sat on his knee. Nineteen-two, I think. No, it must have been nineteen-three. Year the drought broke, anyhow."

The girl Mora said, "It is mind talk."

"What do you mean, mind talk?" said Arch. "You better have another rum. Gets cold out here after sundown."

"We will partake gratefully," said Leri. He held out his milk tin. "I am grateful. Now, mind talk is when I send the thought from my mind to yours. We do not need sound waves."

"Or ears either, hey," said Arch. "Would you like another drink, miss?"

"Call me Mora," said the girl, and giggled in mind talk.

"Well, why can't me and Uncle Angus do it then?" asked Arch.

"You can. Everybody can, if the channel is opened," said Leri, waving his tin of rum. "It has been done with earth people before. One of our people found his saucer broken down in Siberia ..."

"Where's that?" said Angus.

"It is a place in Russia," said Leri. "He was broken down there for four months before we could get a spare to him. He lived with a level-crossing keeper called Oleg."

"This Oleg. Was he a commo?" asked Arch.

"He was a man very like Angus, except where he lived was very cold instead of very hot. He makes a rum from potatoes called vodka. He drinks it all the time. There is another man called Hiram Knucklebone at a place called Tennessee. He, too, makes the rum, but he calls it moonshine. He is very like your Uncle. I can hear them all now."

"Strike me blue," said Angus.

"Lend me the pannikin a minute, mate, it's my turn for a nip," said Arch.

Mora hiccuped, blushed, and handed him the quart-pot.

"Well, why did you come down, then, if you got mates here already?" said Angus.

"We are on what you call honeymoon," explained Leri. "Mora wanted to meet some of your people. She has never been here before. We have to be careful who sees us. Hup. Pardon. No one will believe you, you see." Leri grinned, and drank from his tin of rum.

Arch thought for a bit. Then he said, "This channel thing. Could you open mine up for me? I'd like to hear the Yank, too. And the other bloke. It seems a long way to be able to hear a bloke."

"Sure," said Leri. He finished his rum and stared at Arch. After a while Arch said "Yeah, you're right." Without opening his mouth. Then he said, "What about Angus?"

"Not me," said Angus. "Lot of bloody nonsense, hearing other blokes. Anyhow, an old blackfeller showed me how to do it years ago, with a fire and a stone."

"That is another way, but just as good," said Leri. He turned to the girl, who was looking a bit glassy by this. "Well, dear, we had better be getting along, if you are ready. It's a long way to go."

It was, too. Arch could see that.

So the bloke shook hands with both of them and Arch gave Mora a nice black opal for a wedding present and she kissed them both goodbye, and they got back in their flying saucer and flew away. Angus kept his hand over his pannikin till the dust settled, and they never saw them again. Arch says, though, he sometimes hears them flying past and says good day. But the story doesn't end there. You see, what with being able to talk to the Yank and the other bloke now, Arch really got to know them well. He found that they both have blokes like the income tax man, though Oleg calls him a commissar and Hiram calls him a revenuer. Blokes that come round with forms to fill in, and wanting money and information till your eyeballs bulge. And Arch says that when you really get to know a bloke, you don't want to fight him. You mightn't agree with him but you can see how he looks at it and he's got a right to see it his way. They settled down to work on this channel opening business, and the last I heard they were working on a Bantu witchdoctor, an old Scotsman on the Isle of Skye who makes his own whisky, a Patagonian fisherman, and an old Chinese farmer in a commune who pinches rice he makes into wine up in the hills. If they succeed, as well they might, we may all wake up one of these mornings and find we've really got one world. The United Nations might find itself out of a job, mightn't it. I don't know what Angus thinks of it all.